STAR WARS
THE HIGH REPUBLIC

A TEST OF COURAGE

JUSTINA IRELAND

ILLUSTRATIONS BY
PETUR ANTONSSON

Disney
LUCASFILM
PRESS

LOS ANGELES·NEW YORK

Printed in the United States of America

First Edition, January 2021

10 9 8 7 6 5 4 3

FAC-020093-21029

ISBN 978-1-368-05730-1

Library of Congress Control Number on file

Reinforced binding

Design by Soyoung Kim and Scott Piehl

Visit the official *Star Wars* website at: www.starwars.com

STAR WARS
THE HIGH REPUBLIC

The galaxy is at peace, ruled by the glorious REPUBLIC and protected by the noble and wise JEDI KNIGHTS.

As a symbol of all that is good, the *Republic* is about to launch STARLIGHT BEACON into the far reaches of the *Outer Rim.* This new space station will serve as a ray of hope for all to see.

But just as a magnificent renaissance spreads throughout the Republic, so does a frightening new adversary. Now the guardians of peace and justice must face a threat to themselves, the galaxy, and the Force itself....

STAR WARS TIMELINE

THE HIGH
REPUBLIC

FALL OF
THE JEDI

REIGN OF
THE EMPIRE

THE
PHANTOM
MENACE

ATTACK OF
THE CLONES

THE
CLONE WARS

REVENGE OF
THE SITH

THE
BAD BATCH

SOLO:
A STAR WARS
STORY

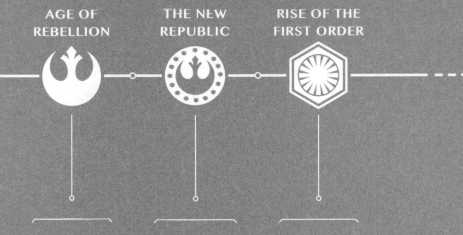

AGE OF REBELLION

REBELS

ROGUE ONE:
A STAR WARS
STORY

A NEW HOPE

THE EMPIRE
STRIKES BACK

RETURN OF
THE JEDI

THE NEW REPUBLIC

THE
MANDALORIAN

RISE OF THE FIRST ORDER

RESISTANCE

THE FORCE
AWAKENS

THE LAST JEDI

THE RISE OF
SKYWALKER

Klinith Da carefully landed the stolen cargo hauler on the edge of the dock while her partner, Gwishi, searched the nearby compartments for the ship manifest. Taking things from the weak was a great way to live, but occasionally it came with its share of hassles, like when dopey officials made life difficult. Normally Klinith didn't worry about such things—as a human woman in a galaxy full of much stronger species, she could handle herself—but they were supposed to be keeping a low profile, and that meant blasting people was unfortunately out of the question.

"Are they going to ask for any official documents?" Klinith asked, pushing her shock of magenta hair out of her face. She caught her reflection in the gleam of a side panel. She looked nothing like she was used to. She'd removed all her piercings and covered her Strike markings—the tattoos that told other Nihil about her crew and her career as a pirate—with the coveralls she wore, but she was not about to change her hair. She was still Nihil, even when she was pretending to be something else.

After a moment she reached into her pocket and threaded her silver wire around and through the holes in her bottom lip. That was a little better, less odd.

"This far out they shouldn't care," the male Aqualish said, his weak command of Basic making the words sound especially snarly. "The Republic doesn't regulate this part of the galaxy. Yet." Like Klinith, Gwishi wore simple coveralls, his Strike markings covered—all but the nasty scar on the right side of his face where he'd taken a blaster bolt to one of his eyes. That still gleamed blue, a jagged line bisecting his bottom right eye and terminating at his tusk. The ink had been added to the still healing wound to show that even though he'd taken a grievous injury, the person responsible was no longer around to repeat the mistake.

The Nihil repaid all their wrongs threefold.

Klinith grabbed both her blaster and her knives, because in stealthy situations knives were sometimes the better option, placing them in her toolbox. Gwishi grabbed his own blaster plus his face mask and a canister of ovax gas, which he placed into his tool kit along with the rest of his gear. The gas would be necessary to incapacitate the mechanics on board the *Steady Wing*, a luxury liner they had followed to Port Haileap, a remote outpost on the edge of the Dalnan sector.

The plan was simple. They'd been told to board the *Steady Wing* and sabotage it so that no one on board was left alive. The ship was scheduled to pick up someone important to the Republic on Haileap, and the Nihil needed to let the Republic know they were not welcome in this part of the galaxy.

Not now, not ever. The Republic was bad for business.

Before disembarking Klinith went back and grabbed one more blaster, small enough to tuck into the top of her boot. Sometimes things went wrong and people got hurt. That was Klinith's favorite part.

There was a short walk through thick jungle, the marblewood trees large and covered in blue moss, before the busy docking station came into view. Klinith had purposely chosen an out-of-the-way landing space to allow her and Gwishi to enter undetected. The last thing they needed was too many people asking questions. Manifest or not, less attention was better.

"That's it right there," Gwishi said, pointing to an enormous ship that took up most of the landing yard. The thing was easily ten times the size of the cargo hauler they'd stolen, and Klinith felt a tendril of fear sneak through her as she considered that.

"How in the seven Genetian moons are we supposed to destroy that?" she asked.

Gwishi sighed. "From the inside. You're Nihil. Act like it and stop worrying."

"I'm not," Klinith said. She had no problem with the mission; it just felt more serious than her previous jobs, like she'd been promoted. And if this job was successful, she surely would be. She'd rise within the Nihil, maybe even report directly to Kassav himself.

Klinith and Gwishi were close to the ship, and she grinned with anticipation. Everyone would be talking about the destruction of the *Steady Wing*. "I'm excited. This is going to be monumental. I'm just sad we don't get to smash anything."

Gwishi watched her with unblinking eyes. "Come on, let's go."

The port was teeming with people from many different systems. As the last stop before some of the most dangerous uncharted regions in the galaxy, Port Haileap, like other ports on the edge of what was considered civilized space, was a place for ships to refuel and for people to catch up on news from back home and relax before spending time in a cramped ship. A large landing area stocked with supplies and surrounded by a ring of shops, it was just like most of the outposts Klinith had been to, with the exception of the giant marblewood trees that were visible in the distance, stabbing the violet sky with their green crowns. Humans, Trandoshans, Pantorans, and more weaved among one another in a throng, making their way to the various shops lining the outside edge of the landing zone. Klinith saw a sign advertising gambling down a far hall and her hands itched. It had been a while since she'd had a chance to play rykestra, a popular dice game. But she had more pressing issues than a game of chance.

Klinith and Gwishi made their way up the boarding ramp to the *Steady Wing*. The Republic guards standing at the top of the walkway were laughing over something and paid the pirates no mind as they walked past. They blended in perfectly with the other mechanics walking on and off the luxury liner. Once they were in the ship proper, Gwishi slapped Klinith on the back.

"Too easy," he said. And he was right.

They walked through the hallway, and Klinith felt a familiar anger rising deep in her middle. It was a grand ship, with beautiful golden floors and silver walls that featured a flower-patterned screen that shifted its design every few seconds. She tried to imagine what it would be like to stay on such a fine ship. She couldn't, and that made her angrier than anything else. She couldn't wait to destroy the

Steady Wing and watch its beauty fracture in the emptiness of space.

Klinith followed Gwishi, stopping when he pointed to a plaque on the side of the hallway. The ship was so large that there were maps every few meters to show how to get to different areas.

"That's where I'm headed." Gwishi pointed to a blank spot before patting the heavy tool kit he carried. "I'm going to leave everyone a few surprises. You go and make sure the escape pods aren't any good, either. The last thing we want is survivors. This should be a disaster that will make the *Legacy Run* look like a day at the fair."

Before Klinith could respond, Gwishi turned and started off down the hallway, leaving her to figure out where the escape pods were held. After a few moments puzzling out the map—she wasn't the best reader, and the map seemed purposely confusing—she figured out they were on another deck.

When Klinith arrived where the escape pods were, she discovered she wasn't the only one there. A maintenance droid buzzed around the bay. At her entrance the droid stopped.

"Are you here to sign off on the pods?" the droid asked. It was a little box of a thing, with several arms sticking out at every angle.

"Yes, but we need to upgrade them. Take out the comms and nav systems."

The droid rolled forward and back as it processed her command. "I have no such instructions. I must update my feeds to receive new instructions."

There was a large, heavy hydrospanner on the wall, and Klinith lifted it in her hands, testing the weight. "Oh, I have your updates right here."

She slammed the heavy tool into the top of the droid, again and again, until the droid was little more than random metal parts. Klinith smiled at the destruction all around her.

She'd gotten to smash something after all.

CHAPTER
ONE

Vernestra Rwoh looked at the gleaming ship in the docking bay and contemplated the task before her with a mixture of excitement and dread. Her first mission for the Jedi Council and her first tasking as a Jedi Knight. She had dreamed about this day since she was a Padawan. She had only been a Knight for a short while, and it still felt too amazing to be true.

Even if the assignment was simply keeping a senator's daughter safe. Babysitting seemed below a Jedi Knight. But! Vernestra was not going to let it dampen her spirits.

The luxury liner on the landing zone had been sent

by the Chancellor herself, and it was grand and impressive. It loomed over the other ships in Port Haileap, its bright exterior flashing like a beached mael fish, massively silver and sleek in its curves. The *Steady Wing* boasted sixteen decks, three decorative gardens, an entire games deck, and even a grand dining room that could seat a thousand. The ship was more lavish than anything Vernestra had ever seen before, and Port Haileap was regularly visited by some of the best tour lines—Galaxy Tours, ThrillSpace Travels, and Chandrila Star Lines—in addition to the pleasure yachts flown by ambassadors visiting outlying planets and adventurers set on discovering new planets in the uncharted regions.

The *Steady Wing* was something entirely different. It was a ship fit for an important delegation.

Vernestra adjusted her tabard, the luminous gold design of the scrollwork along the bottom edge marking her as a Knight from the temple at Hynestia. She shifted uncomfortably in the unfamiliar clothing, finer than what she usually wore. Port Haileap was a rough-and-tumble sort of place where Vernestra usually made do with a day uniform of a gold tunic and ivory trousers overlaid with a simple tabard bearing the same gold embroidered design of her temple. Outposts like Port Haileap had no need for pomp and circumstance. The small bit of civilization carved out of the giant marblewood forest existed to help long haulers refuel and resupply, and the attire of a young Jedi Knight was the last thing on the minds of visitors. But this ship was bound for the dedication of Starlight Beacon, the greatest achievement of the glorious Republic, and would be carrying a delegation from nearby Dalna back to Coruscant after the important occasion. She could not show up in plain ivory and embroidery. So there she was, vaguely uncomfortable in her finery.

Just thinking about Starlight Beacon distracted Vernestra from her thoughts about the mission and doing a good job so she would make the Jedi proud. A massive space station, part temple and part way station for the Republic, Starlight Beacon had been under construction for as long as Vernestra could remember. As a youngling, Vernestra had heard her elders speak of how Starlight, as it was more often referred to, would change the galaxy for the better, especially for those planets far from the Core. Better communications, more support from the Republic . . . Starlight

Beacon was going to change everything. The Republic's space station in the wilds of the Outer Rim would serve as a safe haven in the wilderness, a light in the darkness. It would make the galaxy better for everyone. Vernestra was lucky to get a chance to see it for herself.

It made her proud to be a Jedi and glad that the Force had provided such an opportunity for her. She tried not to let pride overwhelm her, as she knew the Force had just as much to do with her good fortune as her own hard work did, but looking at the *Steady Wing* and contemplating the next few weeks, it was difficult.

In her defense, it had been quite a year. Vernestra had undertaken her Jedi trials earlier than most on recommendation from her master and, to the surprise of many, had passed. "Who is she? She's no one special," some of the other Padawans had muttered, and they were right. Vernestra was only a Mirialan girl with a Force gift, and there were hundreds of other Padawans and younglings just like her.

But as far as she knew, she was the only Jedi who had passed her trials on her first attempt at the age of fifteen, when most Padawans were in the early stages of their apprenticeships. And most days rather than feeling arrogant or prideful at being such a prodigy, Vernestra felt a great responsibility to help the galaxy in whatever ways the Force, and the Jedi Council, determined were best. But was it so wrong to take a moment and relish her accomplishments? She closed her eyes and felt the Force flow through all, and contemplated her feelings and the obligations that lay before her. Even now, at sixteen, it seemed like a lot to be a real Jedi Knight. But she would do it as best as she could as long as she was allowed.

She decided it was fine to be happy about this first mission, even if it was just babysitting.

"Hey, stop her!"

The sense of calm shattered and Vernestra opened her eyes to see a maintenance droid chasing a small, dark-skinned human girl riding a scoot speeder built of odds and ends. The girl's hair framed her face in a halo of riotous curls, and she held a brightly shining power crystal in a single gloved hand. The expression of joyous triumph on her face was one that Vernestra knew all too well.

Avon Starros, daughter of Senator Ghirra Starros, was once again up to no good.

Avon had not yet seen Vernestra, and the Jedi used that to her advantage. Vernestra raised her hands, palms flat toward Avon, and pushed with the Force. The girl went flying backward off of her homemade contraption, but instead of letting her fall hard onto the deck, Vernestra kept Avon suspended in the air while the vehicle froze in the middle of the docking bay.

"Avon," Vernestra said sweetly. "What is going on?"

Avon twisted around in midair, her happy expression souring when she spied Vernestra. "Ugh, I thought you were already on the ship."

"No, I decided to take one last walk through the outpost before we left. I can see I am not the only one. What did you do?"

"Nothing! I didn't do anything. By the stars, I don't know why you always think everything is my fault, Vern."

Vernestra gritted her teeth against the terrible nickname. Master Douglas Sunvale called her that, and while she was not about to correct a Jedi Master, she had no such qualms about correcting a girl younger than her. "Please don't call me that." She released her hold on the Force and let Avon fall to the ground, which was not all that far. The scoot speeder, which Avon had no doubt built from materials left unattended around the port, crashed into a nearby stack of shipping crates.

"You are the worst," Avon groaned, splaying her limbs out dramatically on the ground.

"It wasn't that far," Vernestra said, even though it had been a bit mean to let the girl fall.

"I will take that," the maintenance droid said, plucking the crystal from Avon's gloved hand before stomping back the way it had come. Vernestra walked over to Avon and offered her a hand up, but the younger girl just glared at her and picked herself up on her own.

"One day, when I am the galaxy's foremost inventor, I am going to create a device that blocks the Force," Avon said. "And then let's see how you like that."

Vernestra laughed. "Avon, we've discussed this. The Force is all around and inside of us, as well. It isn't like your power crystals. It's impossible to block the Force. Also, why did you take that droid's energy crystal?"

Avon huffed. "It's for an experiment, and it's not like I'm going to tell you, Jedi. I know you'll find a way to ruin it somehow. Besides, can't you just read my mind?" The girl crossed her arms and Vernestra sighed. She and Avon always butted heads. It wasn't because Vernestra didn't like the young girl. Quite the opposite—she found Avon's many inventions and theories to be endlessly fascinating. But Avon did not like to be told no, and she had ended up in Port Haileap precisely for that reason. Her mother, Senator Ghirra Starros, had sent her there, hoping that some time spent on the edge of space would make Avon more appreciative of her life on Coruscant. All it had done was make Avon more determined to do as she pleased, which was usually inventing machines from bits of other things.

There was no real reason for Avon to accompany the delegation to Starlight and then back to Coruscant; her mother hadn't sent for her and she had no official role on the journey, but Master Douglas, the marshal of the outpost, had asked to have Avon accompany them specifically because the Dalnan ambassador's son was twelve, as well. He was hoping that the two would become friends and soften the Dalnans' view of the Republic.

Vernestra was hoping so, too. Mostly because Avon needed a friend.

"Mistress Avon! You are late. If you do not get on board

that ship this instant I will uncouple your linking hoses and then let's see how well your scoot speeder runs."

A pinkish-gold droid as tall as Vernestra stomped over to where they stood. J-6, Avon's protocol droid, was half warden, half nanny, all attitude. She spoke like no protocol droid Vernestra had ever met, and she suspected that Avon had something of a hand in that.

Avon sighed heavily and pushed her unruly hair out of her face before walking over to her scoot speeder and righting it to climb on. "Well, looks like the jig is up. I got it, Jay-Six, no sabotage necessary. You coming, Vern? You don't want to be late."

Vernestra smiled and nodded. She was excited to see Starlight Beacon, even if it meant she would have to work extra hard to keep Avon out of trouble. "Let's go."

As they walked toward the boarding ramp for the *Steady Wing*, Vernestra stumbled and gasped. Avon gave her a sidelong glance. "Everything okay?"

Vernestra put a hand to her chest and looked over to where an Aqualish mechanic was tinkering with an access panel near the boarding ramp. He stared back at Vernestra with three unblinking eyes. His lower right eye was missing, and blue-tinted scar tissue occupied the space instead. There was nothing else about him that was remarkable; he wore the same orange coveralls as every other member of the docking station's maintenance crew.

"I'm fine," Vernestra said, finally, in answer to Avon's query. Vernestra gave the Aqualish man a small smile, and he turned away without reaction, going back to whatever he was doing. Something about the man made Vernestra feel more alert than was necessary, a spiky sensation that she couldn't explain. She was just nervous and excited about the mission to Starlight, since this was her first real Jedi mission and she didn't want to mess it up. That was why she was fixating on random mechanics doing their jobs.

At least, that was what she told herself, even if she didn't truly feel it.

Pushing the strange feeling aside, Vernestra accompanied Avon and J-6 onto the *Steady Wing* and tried to focus on making sure the young girl did not try to escape before departure. Vernestra had her hands full enough without seeing phantoms in every corner of the Force.

Avon boarded the ship, J-6 and Vernestra on either side. Avon couldn't help but stare at the lightsaber on Vernestra's hip. The weapon was powered by a kyber crystal. She'd heard amazing things about them, and the one time she'd seen the Jedi use her lightsaber, the blade had glowed purple with pure energy. Avon had tried to talk Vernestra into letting her examine it more closely, but the older girl had politely refused.

"A Jedi and her kyber are linked through the Force. It sings to me and my spirit returns that call. It's not a mere energy crystal, Avon. I am sorry. But no."

Avon had decided long ago the worst thing about Vernestra was how aggravatingly nice she was. Always apologizing to Avon when she told her no. It was almost as bad as J-6's constant nagging about her clothes.

"Mistress Avon, we must retire to the cabin set aside for you and prepare for dinner. I also have a dress for you that your mother sent along. It will be perfect for the dedication of Starlight, but it has to be altered before we get there," the droid said, all rose-gold annoyance.

"Yes, that is a good idea," Vernestra said. "Although, you should have a good bit of time to alter the dress. Master Douglas said that because of the recent hyperspace disasters we will be spending more time traveling by sublight until we can get to a safe jump point mid-system, and then entering lightspeed to continue our journey. So it would probably be a good idea to get comfortable since we'll be aboard for a long while."

"Oh, that is a delight to hear. This ship is state-of-the-art, unrivaled luxury," J-6 said, her mechanical voice lilting with joy. "I cannot wait to plug in and update my programming. And it's been so long since anyone oiled my sockets." The droid gave Avon a meaningful look, and the girl snorted.

"Last time I tried to give you an upgrade you freaked out."

"That is because you added an entire dictionary's worth of Aqualish curse words to my lexicon! You are a terrible child who is ungrateful and mean."

Avon grinned, because there was no real heat to J-6's words. "Yeah, but think about how great it was when those wine haulers came through and you tried to greet their captain. I didn't even know the Aqualish had a sense of humor, but that crew almost passed out from laughing so hard."

Vernestra's pale green skin darkened several shades, and her dark eyebrows shot so far up her head that they almost reached her hairline. "So that's why Master Douglas had to come down to the docking bay and break up a fight amongst the Aqualish. And they weren't laughing, Avon! Those whistles were Aqualish sounds of challenge. Och, one of these days your mischief is going to have real consequences."

Avon shrugged and waved away Vernestra's admonishment. "Whatever, Vern. You still in charge of making sure I show up to things on this trip?" Avon had planned on staying back at Port Haileap. With the Jedi off to Coruscant and out of the way (the Force always seemed to tell on Avon long before sensors and droid guards did), she'd been planning on finally finishing her latest invention, antigravity shoe inserts. But then J-6 had started packing up her room and said that they were traveling to Starlight Beacon with the diplomatic envoy from Dalna. The only upside was that Vernestra had been stuck with babysitting duty, which meant that maybe Avon would get to see the Jedi's lightsaber again.

"Avon, you are old enough to get to dinner on your own," Vernestra said with a friendly smile, the crinkling of her eyes compressing the designs in the outside corners. Like most Mirialans, Vernestra bore the markings of her family, six tiny black diamonds stacked in two rows of three on the outside corner of each eye. "I'm here to keep you and the ambassador's son safe, not chase you from task to task. At your age I was a Padawan traveling the galaxy with my master. Dressing for a meal surely cannot be beyond your ability."

Avon scowled at Vernestra. "That was only like two years ago. Stop acting like you're so mature," she muttered, realizing full well that talking back was the opposite of being grown up about the matter.

Ugh.

Vernestra didn't seem to mind. She gave a wave and disappeared down the corridor to find her room. Avon turned to J-6.

"I suppose you know where we're staying?"

"Of course, Mistress Avon. That is my job, is it not?"

Avon turned and followed J-6, a little of her bad mood melting away. J-6's response had been less than cordial, and while most would find that distasteful in a protocol droid, Avon was intrigued. A month before, she had uploaded a slow-acting code along with the lexicon of swears (there had been half a dozen) that would gradually strip away the factory programming and let J-6 in essence reprogram herself. Avon had always disliked how droid personalities seemed to be hardwired when they were built, and it seemed fairer to let J-6 decide what kind of droid she wanted to be.

Avon was hoping it was something more interesting than someone who cared way too much about etiquette.

They turned the corner to another corridor, and a human-looking woman with bright pink hair and a pair of greasy coveralls came running toward them. She was so busy looking over her shoulder that she didn't notice Avon and J-6, and before Avon could call out a warning, the woman ran right into the protocol droid.

J-6 did not move, but the woman went stumbling backward before landing hard on her rear end. It was pretty funny, and Avon couldn't help letting out a little laugh.

"Are you okay?" Avon asked. The woman jumped to her feet, refusing to meet Avon's eyes. She had a piece of silver wire woven around her lip, the metal piercing the skin several times like it had been stitched into her face. It was a strange sight, and reminded Avon a bit of how the Mon Calamari liked to hang beads and other jewels from their barbels, those whiskers that grew around their mouths. It was fascinating, and Avon wanted to ask the woman if setting the wire in her face hurt, but the woman's fierce expression didn't exactly invite conversation.

"I'm fine," the woman spit out. "You should teach your droid to watch where it's going."

"And you should *actually* watch where you are going," J-6 said, and Avon's breath hitched. Oh, that was definitely not part of the droid's original protocol programming.

Excellent, this would require further observation.

The pink-haired woman said nothing else, just continued off in the direction she'd been headed. Avon and J-6 went to their quarters to prepare for dinner, the incident quickly forgotten by both the girl and her droid.

Honesty Weft did not want to be in space. He did not want to dress up or eat a formal dinner, and he did not want to be a good Dalnan ambassador's son. But there he was, on the *Steady Wing*, about to do all those things.

No one ever cared much what he wanted.

"Are you going to keep scowling into the mirror, or are you going to finish getting dressed?"

Honesty's father entered his room. Ambassador Weft was already dressed in the plain, formal tunic of the Dalnan ambassadorial corps: a sedate tan tunic with a high collar and matching trousers. Even his boots were unremarkable. The Dalnans were not ones for frivolity, not even the usually ostentatious Pantorans who had made a home on the planet known for its agriculture.

"Perhaps you could pass along my regrets?" Honesty asked hopefully, tugging at the uncomfortable collar.

"That doesn't sound like something a warrior would say," the ambassador said, a smile flitting across his tanned face. He helped Honesty tuck the collar into place, the smile smoothing away into his usual bland expression as he worked. Honesty's father had once explained that the hardest part of being an ambassador was not letting others know what you were thinking. Honesty had tried to match his father's air of polite interest more than once, but his usual scowl always came through.

One more reason he would never be an ambassador.

"I'm not going to be anything since I'm missing my Metamorphosis."

His father sighed, gave Honesty's collar one last pat, and sat on the edge of his son's bed. "This again."

"Yes, this again," Honesty said, not bothering to hide his frustration as he adjusted his formal tunic. "Everyone else is testing into their vocation right now, and I'm here! By the time I get back, everyone is going to be at least an apprentice in their field, and I'll be stuck in the nursery with the rest of the babes."

"There is something to be said for taking one's time," Ambassador Weft said. "Don't always be in a hurry to be the first one out of the gate. Sometimes the first of the herd is just quickest to the slaughter."

"I'm not talking about a stupid farm, I'm talking about my life!" Honesty shouted.

His father stood. "I am not going to spend the entirety of this trip arguing with you about why you are here. Your mother and I made a decision, and we expect you to respect that. Leaving Dalna will give a measure of perspective that will help you no matter what vocation you choose. If you don't want to be considered a babe in the nursery, stop acting like one." His voice was even and calm, even though the words felt to Honesty like a verbal slap. "You are going to be a witness to history. If Dalna joins the Republic we'll get security and safety in our sector of the galaxy. You'll get to see what diplomacy looks like firsthand, and maybe even get to meet the Chancellor. You should appreciate that instead of acting like a spoiled zeftgeist fat from too much grain."

Honesty opened his mouth to argue, but the ambassador was already on his feet and moving toward the door. "Janex and the rest of the delegation will be here momentarily. I expect you to greet them with a smile and words of anticipation, not sulkiness. Do not disappoint me."

With that the ambassador left the room, and Honesty was left with nothing but the angry tears of frustration that streamed down his pale cheeks.

FOUR

Later, after takeoff and some deep meditation, Vernestra walked into the dining room where dinner would be taking place, feeling centered and eager to be on her journey. There were six dining areas located on the ship, but the best, most intimate one had been set aside for the Dalnan delegation, a server droid assured Vernestra. She was chagrined to find she was one of the last to arrive. Master Douglas and his Padawan, Imri Cantaros, were already seated at one end of the table next to a few men and women Vernestra did not recognize. Avon was nowhere to be found, but Vernestra was sure that J-6 would make certain the girl attended the formal affair, so she put those concerns aside and strode toward the table set with an almost impossible number of silver utensils.

"Vern! You're just in time," Master Douglas said with a grin.

Vernestra grimaced. "Master Douglas, I hope you know Avon Starros loves calling me Vern thanks to you. You are rubbing off on her."

Douglas laughed, a hearty sound that made even the dour-faced Dalnans seated to either side of him smile briefly. "I should hope so! The girl is a genius. Avon will be one of the greatest minds of her generation. I would be honored to be counted amongst her influences."

Vernestra smiled and took the seat that the server droid indicated, directly next to Imri. As she settled, Vernestra assessed her dining companions. Master Douglas was a tall human, stocky and effusive. He was chatty and relaxed in his demeanor, nothing like Vernestra's master Stellan had been. Douglas's dark beard grew thick and unkempt across his pale face, and his robes were rarely worn; instead he preferred to wear the simple tunic and trousers of the Outer Rim settlers of planets like Dalna. He did have his lightsaber, as a proper Jedi always would, but that was the only indication of his status. That night he had worn the required tabard of a Jedi Master, the gold scrollwork set against the snowy material impressive even if it was clear it had been hastily unpacked.

"I spent all afternoon looking for it. Luckily, I had ordered another one," Imri whispered conspiratorially to Vernestra. The human boy was from Genetia originally, even though he had spent his youngling years in the main temple on Coruscant. Imri was tall and broad-shouldered, and his hefty frame was a perfect match for his master's. He had pale skin, a mop of golden hair, kind brown eyes, and an uncanny knack for perceiving the feelings and thoughts of those around him.

"Master Douglas is fortunate to have you," Vernestra said with a kind smile.

Imri laughed. "I'm lucky to have him. I still haven't managed to finish reconstructing my lightsaber. And it was so easy the first time I did it! But now, it just feels wrong every time I piece it back together."

"It happens. But don't worry, you'll get it. Did you ever consider asking Douglas to take you to the temple for the empath tests?" Vernestra asked. The capacity to perceive the feelings of others was a rare Force ability, but these were marvelous times. More and more it seemed that the Jedi would spread their light throughout the galaxy and make life better for all. Wasn't that why the Republic had undertaken construction of Starlight Beacon? Because of the benevolence of the Jedi?

Imri shook his head. "It's not the Force, Vernestra, it's just paying attention. Hey, do you think you could tell me a little bit about your trials?" he whispered. "Douglas thinks I should start training for them, but I don't know. I don't feel ready."

Vernestra smiled and leaned in close to Imri. "You have a while. I took mine early because Master Stellan thought I was ready." Imri's hopeful expression fell just a bit, and Vernestra put a comforting hand on his should. "Don't worry, Imri! You have lots of time. Didn't you just turn fourteen?"

"Yes, but . . ." Imri's voice trailed off and he sighed. "I'm ready to be a Knight."

"You'll be ready when the Force says you are," Vernestra said gently.

Imri sighed again. "Yes, Master Douglas says much the same thing. By the way, don't let him forget to introduce you to the Dalnans. They've heard stories about you and they're very excited to meet our local celebrity."

Vernestra felt a flush of happy embarrassment, but Douglas stood and cleared his throat, hearing Imri's words.

"Ah, yes, thank you, my dear Padawan, for the gentle reminder." He chuckled and held out a hand to Vernestra. "Ambassadors Weft, Janex, and Starstriker, please allow me to introduce you to the pride of Port Haileap, Vernestra Rwoh. Vernestra here—we call her Vern for short—is the youngest Padawan to pass her trials in a very long time. She is quite the rising star."

"What exactly happens during the Jedi trials? Is it a test of strength or intellect?" Ambassador Weft asked. The man's face bore deep furrows, as thought he had lived a difficult life. His hair was fiery red and his skin tanned, though not nearly as dark as Avon's. He looked to spend a lot of time out in the warmth of a sun, of which Dalna had two. He and his son were the only humans from his delegation; the rest of the Dalnans were Pantoran, Trandoshan, or Weequay. All wore plain tunics and trousers, their knee-high boots simple and utilitarian. They each bore the same somber expression and carried a small arsenal of blasters, a show of strength that had intimidated other Republic envoys to the planet. There had been a war on Dalna a century or so before, and the population had responded by becoming a formidable culture that trained constantly for battle.

"The trials are both," Vernestra said with a smile, answering the ambassador's question. "They are designed to test an individual Jedi's strengths and weaknesses."

"No two trials are the same," Douglas interjected, clapping the ambassador on the shoulder like they were old friends. "I have heard that your Metamorphosis Trials on Dalna are similar."

"Not quite," said a Pantoran female, Ambassador Janex, with a polite smile. She wore the same khaki uniform as the rest of the Dalnan delegation, the brown material making her blue skin seem even more vibrant. "Our Metamorphosis does test the strengths of our children, but only to prepare them for the harsh realities of life on our planet. They are more job-specific than anything else."

"Yes," agreed Ambassador Weft, his voice even and

soft. "For example, my son Honesty's trials will be focused on hand-to-hand combat since he has expressed interest in joining our military." At the mention of the Metamorphosis, Honesty had looked down at his lap, and Vernestra wondered if he was excited or afraid of his trials. But then Ambassador Weft continued speaking and she turned her attention back to the older man. "He will be tested in his ability to defend himself and survive harsh conditions, both skills necessary to endure battle."

"What need does he have when there hasn't been a proper war for a century?"

Everyone turned to look at Avon and J-6 as they entered, Avon's words making just as much of an impact as her tardiness. "Sorry to be late. I seem to have grown a few centimeters since my last fitting. Avon Starros, daughter of Senator Ghirra Starros. Ambassadors, please let me extend the warmest greetings of the Republic and welcome you aboard this fine vessel sent by my mother."

"This ship was sent by the Chancellor," said Ambassador Janex with an arch of her brow.

Avon smiled politely. "And who do you think it was

that convinced the government to part with the funds? As I am sure you know, my mother is adamant that the Republic should double in size in her lifetime. We are, as the saying goes, stronger together. If Dalna joins the Republic everyone wins. Hopefully you will be able to see that during this trip."

The Dalnan delegation murmured, but Avon said nothing else, just bobbed an answering curtsy.

Vernestra tried not to gape at the young girl. This was an Avon whom Vernestra had never met. The girl's unruly curls had been swept back on each side and she wore so many ruffles that she looked to be half coniferous tree and half confection. Her dress was formed from layers of cream and peach gnostra fiber, an homage to the gnostra bush, the ever-useful natural resource of Dalna. Even though Avon looked like a completely different girl, she still plopped down into her chair, the only empty seat, right next to Honesty Weft, a brown-haired boy with pale freckled skin. He was the spitting image of Ambassador Weft, only their hair color setting them apart.

"We have had battles on our planet in the last century,"

the boy said, his voice quiet and barely intelligible. "The peace of the Republic does not always extend to her planets."

"Or her hyperspace lanes," chimed in Ambassador Janex, taking a long drink of her scarlet gnostra berry wine before she continued. "I have heard the most recent disaster in hyperspace has been thought to be an act of sabotage."

"Of the hyperspace lanes?" Avon asked, reaching for a glass of the same wine. J-6 quickly interfered and poured a tall glass of the pink gnostra berry juice instead, and Avon's scowl was fleeting as she smiled across the table at the delegation.

So the quarrelsome child was still there under all those frills. That somehow made Vernestra glad.

"Yes," Ambassador Janex said, warming to the topic. Her blue cheeks flushed prettily. "The initial destruction of the *Legacy Run* set off a series of cataclysms people are calling Emergences, an eruption of remnants of the wreckage appearing randomly across the galaxy."

"The most notable was in the Hetzal system," Imri said, speaking to the group for the first time. "Master Douglas helped to save a lot of lives."

"Imri is correct. As a Jedi who was called in to deal

with the disaster, I can tell you that the tragedy has been handled," Douglas said with his usual good cheer. "A heartbreaking catastrophe, to be sure, but the Jedi and the Republic came together to handle not just the initial disaster, but the subsequent Emergences, as well. There is nothing to fear now."

Ambassador Janex tapped her lips. "Do we know this for certain? The chatter across the news feeds seems to indicate that even though the Jedi response was quick and efficient, the reason we are still seeing these . . . Emergences . . . is not because the original ship is still breaking up in the hyperspace lanes but because the saboteurs are still on the job."

Master Douglas shook his head. "Trust me, esteemed ambassador. There is nothing to fear. Hyperspace is safe as it always has been, even safer since the Republic undertook the mapping project a century ago."

"So, we will be traveling through hyperspace, then," said Avon.

Douglas nodded. "Eventually. I spoke to the pilot, and most of the in-system access points to the hyperspace lanes are still closed, so we're going to have a slight detour before we jump. It'll add an extra day of travel time, but that just gives everyone an excuse to tour the gorgeous Pantoran-style hanging gardens on deck three instead of working."

The adults around the table laughed, and Vernestra frowned. She didn't like that they would be going into hyperspace, but she couldn't tell if it was her own misgivings about traveling the lanes or the nervousness of the Dalnan delegation. They all looked a bit unsettled after the hyperspace conversation. Douglas had told her that the Dalnans rarely left their home planet and disliked space travel as a whole, so maybe that was where the feeling came from.

The server droids moved closer and began placing the first course in front of everyone. The dishes had just been settled on the tabletop when there was a jolt and then another.

"Oh my," the Pantoran ambassador exclaimed. "A bit of debris, perhaps?"

Douglas grinned, but his smile evaporated too quickly. "Stars," he breathed. He threw out his hands and Vernestra felt like she was being pushed into her seat. That was when she felt the disturbance in the Force.

It was like a blade slicing through her, a sharp edge

made of fear and panic. But it wasn't coming from her companions; it was coming from every other living thing on the ship. There were several large crashes, and then alarms began to blare just as the roof of the dining room ripped away to reveal the stars beyond.

"Hold on!" Master Douglas yelled, reaching out with the Force to hold everyone at the table in place. The emergency bulkhead overhead, a metal curtain made of interlocking pieces, began to close before screeching to a halt, leaving several meters open. The doors to the dining room slammed shut at the same time, leaving them with only the air that was very quickly escaping into space.

"It's stuck!" Avon yelled. J-6 stood behind the girl, holding her in place. The vacuum of space pulled all the available atmosphere out of the ship, creating a sucking motion that made Vernestra's eyes water. Droids flew out into the black, as well as dishes and tablecloths, and Vernestra threw her own energy into keeping everyone at the table so they would not also be pulled out into the unforgiving void. But if they did not manage to close the bulkhead, it would not matter. They would very soon suffocate.

"Vern, you need to clear out that edge. Do you think

you can do that?" Master Douglas had his eyes closed, and sweat beaded on his forehead from the effort of keeping everyone where they were.

A quick glance up and Vernestra's heart sank. It looked impossible. How would she keep from being sucked out into space like everything else?

"I'm on it," Vernestra said, pushing aside her doubts and releasing her hold on the people at the table, leaving that task to Master Douglas. She stood, only the Force keeping her from flying away. Debris from odd corners of the room still flew past every now and again.

Vernestra looked up toward the bulkhead again and saw what Master Douglas had meant. A chair had lodged in the bottom edge of the track, and in order for the bulkhead to close it would have to be removed.

She pulled out her lightsaber, took a deep breath, and released her hold on the Force, letting herself be sucked out toward space.

Vernestra could not catch her breath as she was pulled along by the current of air exiting the dining room. A plate flew past her head and she leaned back to avoid it, which sent her into an end-over-end tumble. A brief second of panic, and then Vernestra twisted and corrected her flight, only to slam into the edge of the bulkhead as she did, scrabbling for purchase as she tried to stand.

Flying was much, much easier in theory than practice.

"You're doing great, Vern," called Avon, and Vernestra glanced down at the people below. Avon looked so small and scared, and the boy Honesty was not much better. Vernestra felt a surge of motivation.

She was a Jedi, and the Jedi protected all life. She could do this.

Her faith in her abilities brought forth a fresh burst of energy, and the Force was there, all around her. It filled her and flowed through her as she ran across the bulkhead, lightsaber drawn, the lavender light as steady as her intent. There was not a shred of doubt in her now, and she slashed at the chair blocking the track, shaving off a bit of the bulkhead in the process.

As the metal began to move, Vernestra ran along the shutter, using her lightsaber to liberally slice through any other debris that threatened to jam up the shield. She remained a few centimeters above the metal, and when it finally slammed close, silencing the roaring wind and sealing the breach, she did a backflip and slowly lowered herself to the ground. By the time her boots hit the floor everyone was talking at once.

Master Douglas held up his hand, and the noise died down. "We need to evacuate."

"What is happening?" demanded Ambassador Weft, his eyes bulging with panic.

"I believe something hit the *Steady Wing*. An Emergence, perhaps," Douglas said. He reached his hand out toward the exit door, which had sealed itself when the bulkhead refused to close. He touched the emergency release next to the door, but nothing happened. When that did not work, he pulled out his lightsaber and cut through the door, using the Force to shove the pieces out into the hallway.

"We need to move," Douglas said. "Vern, lead the way!"

CHAPTER
FIVE

Imri could swear his heart was about to pound right out of his chest. *It is as the Force wills it,* he thought, taking a deep breath and letting it out. If they survived this trial it would be because the Force wished it to be so, and that certainty gave Imri a measure of calm. He trusted the Force just like Master Douglas said he should. Imri could be confident as long as Master Douglas was by his side. Even if he had asked Vernestra to lead the way and not Imri, his trusted Padawan.

He took another deep breath and ran along with the rest of the group.

The once impressive hallway was crowded with droids and panicked passengers. Imri did not know who they were, but he figured they must be other important passengers invited to the reveal of Starlight Beacon by the Chancellor. Everyone ran down the hallway toward the escape pods, and the crowds were so thick that Imri had to press against the wall to get past the knot of people.

"This is no good," Master Douglas said, turning back toward the group. "There's no way to get to the escape pods this way."

"The pods are gone," croaked a beautifully dressed Mon Calamari man. "You have to get upstairs to the next deck. There are none left down here."

"How can that be?" Ambassador Weft said with a frown. "This ship has less than half of the passengers it can accommodate."

A cracking sound began to echo through the ship, along with far-off booms that caused everyone in the hallways to scream, duck, and scatter. Master Douglas frowned just as alarms began to wail an alert.

"Get back!" he yelled.

There was a push to the middle of Imri's chest, and

he went flying backward along with Honesty, Avon, and Vernestra. Imri fell into the droid, J-6, and groaned.

"Excuse you," she said, a bit snippily for a droid.

Imri did not have a chance to respond. He stared in surprise as a bulkhead slammed shut, separating them from Master Douglas and the adults of the Dalnan delegation.

"Father!" Honesty said, jumping to his feet and running up to the barrier. He pounded his fists against the metal.

GO. SAVE YOURSELVES, Imri heard inside his head.

"Did you do that?" Avon demanded, eyes wide as she stared at Vernestra. The Mirialan shook her head, the motion causing her hair to come loose from the fastener holding it back.

"It was Master Douglas," Imri said, climbing to his feet. "He pushed us backward so we wouldn't be trapped by the bulkhead. We have to go back the way we came."

Honesty rested his forehead against the barrier for a moment before straightening, dashing away tears as he did so. "Then let us go," he said, his jaw clenched. His mop of brown hair had been tousled and his pale brown tunic was ripped along the high neckline, but that was the only sign that they had just been through a maelstrom. When Imri reached for him with his senses, a habit that helped him understand how other people were feeling, he felt nothing, just a tightly controlled set of emotions. Either the boy was still in shock, like Avon, whose feelings were in such disarray that she'd settled on annoyance, or he had locked down his terror so tightly that Imri could sense nothing through the Force.

Master Douglas had urged Imri to get better at talking to people, not just to suss out what was happening by way of the Force, but Imri couldn't help it, most especially when everything but the Force felt chaotic and wrong.

If only Master Douglas were there to walk Imri through the confusion he was feeling. But he was on the other side of the barrier. The elder Jedi had given them all a chance to survive.

Their motley crew ran down the hallway, Avon in the lead. She stripped off her skirt as she ran, revealing leggings and boots underneath. Imri was not surprised, the girl always seemed to be prepared for anything.

Avon skidded to a stop in front of a badly damaged hatch, scowling.

"How about a little Force help?" Avon said, gesturing to the crumpled door. The metal had been pushed to one side so the door would be impossible to open without a welding torch or some sort of heavy gravity hammer.

Imri was closest, so he drew his lightsaber and slashed through the metal. He tried to use the Force to push the remaining bits out of the way, just as Master Douglas had earlier, but his control was slippery. It was hard to reach the Force when all you could think about was whether or not your master had made it out alive.

Vernestra holstered her lightsaber before gesturing toward the door without a word, and the pieces folded inward, creating space for Avon and J-6, who wasted no time making their way through the door. Honesty followed at a jog, and when Imri made to go next, the pressure of a hand on his shoulder stopped him. "Imri," Vernestra said. "It's going to be all right. All is as the Force wills it."

Imri nodded, but her words did nothing to chip away at the numb feeling that was growing in his heart. But there was no time for worry; they still had to escape the ship.

They ran down the hallway, past game rooms and a jewelry shop, searching for a way up or down, anything to get to another deck with escape pods. This deck was full of entertainments for passengers, but it was short on pods, and Imri was beginning to think that they would never find a lift or a staircase to the other floors when they came upon an entrance to a hangar.

"We should try there," Vernestra said, pointing to the sealed door.

"How is it all of these doors have been destroyed?" Avon asked, frowning. "It's almost like someone doesn't want us to make it off of this ship."

Vernestra did not wait for Imri to try to open the door this time. She reached out and crumpled the metal like a giant dinner napkin. Avon was the first one through, as usual, but this time Vernestra was right behind her.

"Avon, quit rushing into places without checking first," she said.

Imri waited for Honesty and J-6 to go through the door before he followed. When he entered the hangar, a cramped area with only a single maintenance shuttle, his eyes widened.

"Whoa," he said. Someone had hacked the service droids to pieces. There looked to be a trio of them that had been dismantled, their components left strewn about.

"I don't think this was an Emergence," Vernestra said, drawing her lightsaber and holding it out before her. "Someone wanted to make sure no one could leave."

"So, we're doomed," Honesty said, his voice flat. "We should've known better than to travel amongst the stars. We should have welcomed our ends in the dining room."

Avon gave the boy a look somewhere between disbelief and disgust. "There's always hope. The maintenance shuttle is better than nothing. But we need to hurry up. Look." She pointed to where the wall had begun to open up, revealing the darkness of space just outside, beyond a shimmering barrier. The emergency hull breach protocol that protected ships in case of an emergency was beginning to fail. "That is a secondary layer and only meant to last long enough to secure passengers in bulwarked parts of the ship."

"And with the damage we saw in the dining room, even the bulwark areas are compromised," Vernestra finished. "We don't have time to be picky. I can feel Master Douglas . . . fading."

"Me too," said Imri, voice quiet. It was a terrible feeling, and he wanted to cut himself off from the Force to avoid knowing that somewhere on the ship his mentor was fighting for his life, and losing.

"What does that mean?" Honesty asked.

No one answered him.

"This shuttle seems to be mostly operational," J-6 called. Avon dashed over to the droid, and the rest of the group followed her. As luxurious as the *Steady Wing* had been, the maintenance shuttle was the opposite. White interior with gray seats positioned along each wall, and pilot and copilot seats up front. There were cabinets full of tools and hopefully a few supplies, foodstuffs and water to last until they could make it to a way station. It was a tight fit once inside, and Imri stood near the back, uncertain what to do. Vernestra moved toward the pilot's seat, but Avon was already there, flipping switches and turning knobs.

"You know how to fly?" Imri said, skeptical. As a Padawan he had not started pilot's training yet, and Avon was at least two years younger than him. It made him feel uncertain and a little envious that the girl knew what to do, even without the Force to guide her.

"I stole my first escape pod when I was six, while with

my mom on a diplomatic trip to Mon Cala. Trust me, I know how to fly." Avon grinned. The smile did not erase the way her hands shook or the perspiration sparkling along her hairline. Imri could sense her fear but admired that it did not stop her from doing what needed to be done. They were all scared—watching a ship break apart and leave only the stars beyond was not normal—but they were all dealing with it in their own ways.

"I do recommend buckling up, though," J-6 said, lowering herself into one of the seats along the wall and clicking restraining straps into place.

Vernestra sat in the copilot's seat next to Avon. Imri strapped in across from J-6 while Honesty sat next to him. Imri smiled at the younger boy.

"It's going to be okay," he said.

"It's already not okay," Honesty said, and there was so much conviction in his words that Imri just looked down at his hands.

"Everything seems operable, but I'm getting an error with the shielding," Avon called from the front. "There's going to be a lot of debris as we detach," she said gravely. "So hold on to your butts."

Imri swallowed hard. Without shields a random piece of the *Steady Wing* could spell their doom. They weren't out of danger yet.

"I can help with that," Vernestra said. "Um, the debris. Not the holding of butts."

Avon laughed. "Well, yay for the Force."

There was a jolt as the shuttle detached, and then they were speeding away from the slowly destructing *Steady Wing* and into the darkness of space. Imri closed his eyes and tried to send an emotion through the Force to his master, to let the man know everything he had meant to him as a teacher. He concentrated, shaking with the effort of reaching out.

But the Jedi, and the rest of the Dalnan delegation, was already gone.

CHAPTER
SIX

Avon gripped the yoke harder than necessary as she piloted the maintenance shuttle away from the much larger ship. She should've let Vernestra fly. Everyone knew that the Jedi were expert pilots, the Force giving them an edge over most everyone else. At least, that's what the stories said. And after living with Vernestra at Port Haileap, Avon had learned that the stories about the Jedi should be believed. Especially after that maneuver in the dining room. Who but a Jedi would *let* themselves be pulled out toward space to close a bulkhead? No one Avon knew.

Avon should have let Vernestra fly, but when J-6 had pointed out the lone functioning shuttle, Avon had run into it and jumped into the pilot's seat because it was something to do besides thinking about disintegrating ships and Jedi Masters using the Force to save her life.

Poor Douglas. Avon had liked him. He'd called her clever once and handed her a sour berry sweet from his pocket. It seemed desperately unfair that he would meet his end in such a completely random, illogical way. What were the chances of a ship breaking apart in straight space? Hyperspace lanes could be risky, especially the closer one got to the Outer Rim. But they were mostly safe as long as everyone followed the rules.

There was no logical explanation for this, and that was what Avon hated the most.

Next to her Vernestra jumped, and in the back Imri let out a moan. Avon twisted around in her seat to look at the Padawan before turning to the Jedi next to her.

"What's going on? What happened?"

"The ship, it's gone," Vernestra said. Avon wondered what she meant, and then the proximity sensors began to scream. Through the viewport chunks of debris went

whizzing past, and there was only one explanation Avon could think of for such a phenomenon.

The *Steady Wing* had exploded.

Avon's heart clenched at the knowledge Master Douglas was gone forever. It wasn't fair. If the Force was really guiding everything, how could good people like Master Douglas die so stupidly?

"Are you okay?" Vernestra asked, startling the younger girl. She watched Avon with wide-eyed concern, and Avon dashed away the tears that had managed to spring free.

"I'm great. Are you ready?" Vernestra raised an eyebrow, and Avon blew out an impatient breath. "Vern, you said you were going to use the Force to keep us safe. The shields on this model are not very strong, and we have to get through that, which seems to be getting worse by the minute." Through the viewport the way before them was littered with pieces of the ship, and other things besides. Avon tried not to look at the debris too closely. She was afraid if she did, the random bits of trash would resolve into people and recognizable things.

Avon pushed the image aside. *Focus on the now. Control your impulses, Avon.* The voice in her head was her mother's.

Senator Ghirra Starros had never met a problem she couldn't solve, and even if Avon worked very hard to be nothing like her mother, it was still a valuable trait to have.

"One foot in front of the other," she muttered.

The proximity alarms continued to blare, the sound pulling Avon from her wayward thoughts. She had really had enough of alarms for one day.

The shuttle shuddered, jostling everyone aboard. Behind Avon, Imri and the Dalnan boy, Honesty, shifted. "Is that supposed to happen?" called Imri.

"No, this is just our day getting worse," Avon said. "The shields don't seem to be working at all."

"I can handle it," Vernestra said, closing her eyes and leaning back in the seat.

Avon took a deep breath and let it out, and then the maintenance shuttle was deep in the debris field.

Avon had been obsessed with theoretical disaster for years. Every time she and her mother had traveled on official Republic business, Avon had taken great joy in relaying the facts and risks associated with long-haul space travel and hyperspace to anyone who would listen. There were hundreds of logs about what happened when a ship began to break apart in space, most recently with the *Legacy Run*. As reports came in Avon had been fascinated with them, not because of the loss of life, which was terrible, but because of wanting to understand how the disaster had happened and learn to prevent others like it. Avon believed that tech held the answer to most every problem, and even if it seemed like she was just looking for trouble, she was actually looking for answers.

The answer for the debris field caused by a rapidly disintegrating ship was proximity alarms, which was why every craft was supposed to have them, even maintenance shuttles that usually stayed near the larger vessels they were used to maintain. But warning systems were only half the equation, and without any kind of shielding, the ship would be vulnerable to breach. Avon's heart pounded with worry. Vernestra looked tired, her closed eyes and steady breathing not able to erase the lines of fatigue around her eyes. Hopefully, she would be able to help them get past the worst of the danger.

Avon took another deep breath and accelerated.

The first bit of debris swirled around them, moving away and to the side as they sped past. Some of the tightness in

Avon's chest loosened. Everything was fine; they'd avoided the worst of the catastrophe.

But then a screeching came from the top of the shuttle, the sound of something big scraping along the outside hull. Avon flicked her eyes over to Vernestra, whose green skin was liberally dotted with perspiration. "Sorry," she whispered. Her eyes were squeezed shut with concentration, scrunched so hard that the tiny diamonds tattooed around the outside of each eye had nearly disappeared.

Vernestra was fading, even if she wouldn't admit it.

The Jedi's stubbornness prickled at Avon in an annoying way, because it was something she could admire, if there were time. Instead she turned back toward the readout.

"Hey, Imri, you think you can help? Keeping all of the bits from wrecking our ship?" Vernestra called.

"I can try," Imri said, a quaver in his voice, and Avon felt bad for him. He'd just lost his master a few minutes before. Did grief hinder a Jedi's ability with the Force? She certainly hoped not.

Avon kept her eyes fixed on the readout from the proximity sensors. "I mean, if you don't we're joppa stew, if you get my drift." There was nothing worse than joppa stew, in Avon's opinion.

"I can do it," he said, even if he didn't sound completely convinced.

If neither Vernestra nor Imri could be their fail-proof shield, Avon would have to improvise.

Good thing she excelled at that.

Avon did a few brief calculations in her brain. It would be risky, but she thought she could make it.

It was probably for the best that they hadn't eaten dinner.

"Hold on," she called.

"Oh joy," said J-6.

Avon gave the tiny craft full power and swung the yoke hard to the left. The maintenance shuttle began to tilt like a ride she'd once been on at the Republic Fair, and two seconds later she yanked the control back the other way and then forward. The shuttle shifted wildly, sliding between two large pieces of the ship before tilting upward to avoid another bit of refuse.

"Where did you learn to fly?" asked Honesty.

"Simulator," Avon said. "But I've been borrowing real ships to learn to fly since I was six."

"She means 'stealing,'" J-6 said.

"I don't feel so well," Imri muttered.

"We're almost through," Avon said. "Vern, you hanging in there?"

"Yes." Her voice was little more than a whisper, and the tension and worry bloomed once more in Avon's middle. What happened to a Jedi who used the Force too much? Did they get sick? Maybe Vernestra would wither away into an old lady before Avon's eyes, her life spent in a great, final act.

That thought actually scared Avon more than the shuttle being pierced by space trash. But the Jedi were mighty, their weapons powered by a nearly limitless energy source. Vernestra would be fine.

She had to be.

Avon, who usually loved discovering the answers to her questions, decided she did not want to know the solution to this quandary, and turned her attention back to weaving through the last bit of the debris.

She accelerated and swerved before rolling the craft to

avoid hitting one last piece of wreckage with the fragile wings of the shuttle. And then the proximity sensors were quiet and the alarming scarlet display went green.

"We didn't die," said Honesty. Avon swallowed a sigh. She wondered if she was still expected to be diplomatic with the boy since he was most likely the last member of the Dalnan delegation.

That was when it hit Avon: All those people, everyone on the ship. They were all gone. Maybe some of them had gotten to escape pods, but she didn't think so. Douglas and the Dalnan ambassadors were gone, too, including Ambassador Weft. Avon tried to imagine what she would do if she'd had to leave her mother to the mercy of a disintegrating luxury passenger ship.

She didn't like the way her heart clenched at the thought. Poor Honesty.

"Well, I would not have died," J-6 said to no one in particular. "I would have just floated through the galaxy, circuits slowly freezing, a rescue beacon blinking until my systems shut down. So, yes, I do suppose this is better than that."

Avon twisted to look at her droid. Okay, maybe the

self-actualization programming was working a little too well.

"Good job," Avon said to Vernestra as she turned back to the controls. She began flipping switches and checking systems, but the more she checked the further her heart sank.

It looked like they weren't quite out of danger just yet.

Honesty Weft was not going to cry.

He blinked hard and took deep breaths, just as he'd been taught in his defensive arts classes. Centered. Grounded. A warrior remained calm even in the midst of chaos.

This, of course, was much more than any Dalnan warrior had ever had to experience. After all, there had not been a war on Dalna in over a hundred years. And Dalnans kept their fights, when they did happen, planetside, where there was air.

He hadn't even wanted to come on this trip. He'd tried to stay home, to study for his Metamorphosis instead. Honesty wanted to be a combat medical officer, and it was some of the most difficult training around. But his mother had pushed him to accompany his father on his ambassadorial trip, and as always his father had agreed with her.

"Before you decide on a career path, it's important to try a number of things," she'd said while packing his bags. "Travel is how an academic, and a warrior, broadens their horizons. Travel, Honesty. Go see the galaxy with your father, and bring me back stories for the family history. Have an adventure! It's what boys your age are supposed to want to do, not train for a war that is never going to come."

Honesty had been annoyed that his mother, who had grown up on far-off Corellia and come to Dalna after meeting his father at university, had been so nonchalant about leaving the planet and hurtling through the stars. Most Dalnans never even left the temperate zones, and fewer still ever left the planet.

And now Honesty could understand why.

After the mad dash through the remnants of the *Steady*

Wing—a whole ship, just gone!—the shuttle was quiet for a very long time. It didn't feel like they were moving at all. The droid hummed a strange tune to herself, the boy next to Honesty stared at his hands as though waiting for something to appear there, and the Jedi with the green skin, a Mirialan, snored loudly as she slept. But no one talked, not even the girl from the Republic, who seemed like she was having fun more than anything else.

Honesty took another deep breath, and a sharp pain stabbed his middle. Why had he argued with his father? Why couldn't he just be a good and dutiful son? What if he never saw his father again, never got a chance to tell him he loved him and that he was sorry for being disobedient?

Honesty was trying very hard not to panic, but he could feel the hysterical tears creeping ever closer. And when he closed his eyes, all he saw was his father's face, terrified and resigned, as some unseen power shoved that all to the wrong side of the emergency barrier.

"Are you okay?" asked the boy next to Honesty. Imri Cantaros, the Padawan. The boy looked less like a Jedi, or at least what Honesty had imagined the Jedi to look like, and more like the farmers who tilled the lands back home.

He was more than a head taller than Honesty and thick where the Dalnan boy was lanky. But his face was incredibly kind, his eyes shining with concern.

"This is battle. I'm fine," Honesty said, spitting the words out so his voice wouldn't waver. Centered. Strong. Grounded.

Was his father disappointed in him in that final minute? Did he think he was still being petulant? The thoughts raced through Honesty's mind, and he breathed through the emotions that threatened to overwhelm him.

Imri watched him for a long time before nodding a little. "I'm sorry about your father."

Honesty blinked and turned back to the other boy. "What are you talking about?" In his chest, the small flame of hope that his father was still alive flickered as Imri spoke.

Imri flushed and cleared his throat. "No one survived but us. Everyone else is . . . gone."

"You can't know that."

"Of course he can know that. He's a Padawan, which is sort of like an apprentice Jedi. And the Jedi have the Force, which connects all living things." The brown girl—Avon was her name—turned around and gave Honesty a look he didn't care for. He wasn't stupid, but this girl seemed to think he was a bit thick, from the expression on her face. "Besides, the chances of anyone surviving that are . . . not good." She stopped herself, and her dismissive expression melted into one of sadness. "I'm sorry about your father. My mother said nothing but good things about him in the holo she sent, and she doesn't really like anybody."

Tears pricked Honesty's eyes, and he looked down before they could fall. Ah. Now he knew why Imri had been staring down at his hands. It was easier to hide the fact that you were crying if no one could see your face.

"I'm sorry about your father, as well," Honesty said to the boy next to him, his voice thick.

"He wasn't my dad. He was my master," Imri said, but there was anguish lacing his words.

"What did your master do?" There weren't many Jedi on Dalna, and the ones who were there kept to themselves, only stepping in when asked, not like the ones Honesty had met from Port Haileap.

"He taught me what it meant to be a good Jedi, and how to be more in tune with the Force."

Honesty nodded. "That sounds a little like what a parent does."

Imri's expression fell, his pain becoming even more apparent. "Yeah, I guess so."

They both fell quiet once more, and as they flew through the unrelenting blackness of space, the only sound came from the droid as she continued humming to herself. Honesty looked around and realized that he was indeed having an adventure.

And he did not like it one bit.

When Vernestra woke it was with a start. She didn't remember falling asleep, but her body hummed in the way it always did after using the Force heavily. She wasn't exhausted, but there was still a hollowness in her body that was partly hunger and partly the aftereffects of using the Force. Even though she meditated regularly, it was rare that she was required to wield so much power at once. Fighting against the natural vacuum of space had not been easy.

When she was a youngling she'd often reached for the Force, once she learned how, just to feel that thrill, that calm sensation of the galaxy and all the life and energy moving through it. When she became a Padawan she found herself reaching for the Force every night before bed during her meditation, like putting on an extra-comfortable tunic after a long day of hard work. She would often drift off after such meditation, lulled by a sense of rightness and peace.

This sleep had not been that kind of rest. Vernestra stretched as she woke, body aching, head pounding. She'd tested her limits, helping Douglas keep the ship together, pushing away the debris field as they fled the wreckage of the *Steady Wing*.

Douglas. A jab of sorrow lanced through Vernestra as she thought of the Jedi Master. He would return to the cosmic Force that connected all things in the galaxy. Vernestra would feel that connection, and the echo of Douglas, every time she meditated before bed. The cosmic Force was calm and helped give a Jedi wisdom and guidance. That was what happened to all living things when they died, but that didn't minimize the ache of loss Vernestra felt when thinking about the other Jedi. He'd been the first to welcome her to Port Haileap and to congratulate her on passing her trials at such a young age.

"When I was your age I was still trying to figure out the Third Cadence, Vern. You're an amazing Jedi, and I'm proud to get a chance to work with you before you end up on the Council," he'd said with a belly laugh that had made Vernestra feel warm and welcomed.

And now he was gone.

"Imri," Vernestra said, turning around. The Padawan's grief tinged the air around him, leaching into the Force and pulling Vernestra from her seat and to his side. She was no empath—Imri was far more sensitive to the emotions of others than she was—but it was impossible to ignore his pain in the small space of the shuttle.

"I'm sorry, did I wake you?" he said, looking up as Vernestra sat to his left.

"No, I was done resting. How are you?"

"Awful," he said, a tear falling down his cheek and then another following. "But I can feel him a little when I reach for the Force, and that makes it a bit better."

Vernestra put her arm around the boy's shoulders and pulled Imri in for a hug. "When I was a youngling, one of our older masters died while in the middle of meditation. Most of us felt him pass, and while we still missed him, it helped to know that he had gone peacefully and happily. I hope you feel the same when you reach for Douglas."

Imri looked up to meet Vernestra's gaze directly. "Do you think he went peacefully?"

Vernestra grimaced. She could still feel the echo and fear of the ship exploding, the lives lost in that moment of disaster. "No, but I do think he went knowing he had saved us. He died doing what a Jedi should always do: put the will of the Force, the protection of all life, beyond ourselves."

Imri nodded, tears still sliding down his pale cheeks. Honesty Weft sat on his right, dry-eyed and solemn. The boy's sadness seemed like a feeble thing in comparison with the Padawan's grief. But everyone mourned in their own way, and perhaps it hadn't yet sunk in that his father and the rest of the Dalnan delegation were gone. Vernestra did not know the boy well enough to do much more than reach out and squeeze his hand, and even that caused him to startle in surprise.

"I'm sorry about your father," she said, voice soft.

"Thank you," he mumbled, and even though she

wanted to do more, she decided it was best to leave it alone for now.

"Hey, Vern," called Avon. "Could you come here real quick?"

Vernestra climbed to her feet and returned to the cockpit, which was all of a couple of steps away from the passenger area. "What's going on?"

"Okay, so, you know how I said that the shuttle didn't have any shields? Well, that isn't all. I've been trying to bring the comms up since we cleared the debris field, and I've got nothing, not even static."

Vernestra frowned. "Even a maintenance shuttle should have the bare necessities. Navigation, comms, maybe even a hyperdrive."

"We have half a hyperdrive," called J-6 from the back.

Vernestra crossed the shuttle to where J-6 perched over a hole in the floor. The droid had opened up the engine maintenance hatch and was tut-tutting over the various components that made the shuttle go.

"What are you doing?"

The droid pointed to what looked to be a smashed bit

of machinery. "Investigating. It's part of my central programming, though I usually only use it when trying to track down Avon."

"Jay-Six is a repurposed bodyguard droid," Avon called from the front. "My mom thinks nanny droids are a waste of credits, because you outgrow them so quickly."

"Your mom gave you a bodyguard droid as a nanny?" Honesty asked in disbelief.

Avon sighed. "When you meet her, you'll understand."

"Back to the shuttle," Vernestra said.

"Right," Avon said while J-6 continued to scan the engine and other systems. "We also don't have any navigation or maps or, well, anything that we would need to actually figure out a place to go."

"And this hyperdrive won't be able to be brought online," J-6 said finally, shutting the hatch and straightening. "It looks like someone purposely sabotaged this. It is only by sheer luck that this shuttle is even able to fly."

"That is not encouraging," Honesty muttered.

"I'm not sure hyperspace is safe, no matter what Master Douglas thought," Vernestra said with a frown. "There's still the chance we could run into an Emergence." She pushed back a lock of dark hair that had come loose from her fastener and sat in the copilot's chair once more. "How could everything be offline?"

"Sabotage," J-6 said, her words causing a long silence as everyone mulled that over.

"It's really the only answer that correlates to what we saw. There were explosions, one right after another," Avon said. "If it was an Emergence we wouldn't have had a chance to escape. The ship would have gone all at once, just kablooey."

Vernestra took a deep breath and let it out. Avon was right, even if *kablooey* was not the most sensitive way to describe a ship being destroyed.

"You think someone may have planned the attack on the *Steady Wing*?" Imri asked, blond brows pulled together in a frown.

"The odds of a collision with an unknown object while traveling through realspace are very low given the current level of ships' systems designed to prevent such an occurrence, and the chances of several systems on any given shuttle failing all at once are even lower," the droid said dryly. "I can show you the math if you'd like. How are you at Gherillian theoretical proofs?"

Vernestra glanced at Avon, who looked entirely too happy at the bad news. But as soon as she noticed Vernestra watching her, Avon's delighted expression smoothed into something closer to concern. Avon was not the type to delight in harm. Vernestra had a sneaking suspicion the girl really had altered the protocol droid's basic commands.

"Jay-Six is right," Avon said. "But that's not the problem right now. I don't have a place to go, and I have no way of knowing how to get there. We don't have an infinite amount of fuel. The atmospheric levels are good for now, assuming there are some basic supplies in those cabinets. After about another day of flying, things will be . . . not good."

"Our options are simple," J-6 said. "We know what planets exist in the Haileap system. Since we did not jump, it stands to reason we did not travel far. We can either try for Haileap or see if there is something closer. My almanac indicates that there are a few habitable options, although none that will be ideal."

"Without navigation, any guess is as good as another," Avon said with a shrug.

"I could maybe try wayfinding," Imri said, voice hesitant. "Through the Force. Master Douglas was showing me how it is done." Seeing Avon and Honesty's confused expressions, the boy elaborated. "I, um, should be able to detect someplace that has a lot of life, and if there are creatures living there on the planet it should be safe enough for us, as long as I have a good idea of what I am looking for. Right, Vern?"

"Yes," Vernestra said, nodding. "Good idea." It was a long shot. She had only heard a few stories of wayfinding. It was something mostly done by seasoned Jedi Masters who had practiced the skill their entire lives. But she hoped giving the boy a task would help him break through some of the despair of losing his master. Sometimes distractions were helpful.

"Okay, since the nav unit is out, I guess I can just turn the ship until we're pointed in the right direction?" Avon said, doubt lacing her words.

Imri nodded. "Yes, that should work." He closed his eyes and began to breathe evenly, meditating the way all younglings were taught in their first weeks at the temple. Momentous tasks like reaching across great distances always worked better when a Force user was calm and centered, and after the events of the past few hours they were all understandably on edge.

There was still a jangling in Vernestra's head that made her think it was not a good idea for her to try to use the Force right now, not unless she wanted another unscheduled nap. She still felt wrung out from her earlier efforts.

Imri closed his eyes and reached through the Force. But there was something off about his technique, and Vernestra walked back to where Imri sat and took his hand.

"Imri, focus," she said, closing her eyes and reaching out to him through the Force. This kind of connection was mostly passive; joining with the Force was natural and right. They were all part of the living Force, as well as the cosmic Force, and reaching out to the living energy actually quieted some of Vernestra's exhaustion. It could sometimes be too easy for Jedi to get lost in the great possibilities of the Force, and younglings were often taught to remember their own body's needs as a way to anchor their thoughts. Spending too long in the Force could feel luminous, but bodies were crude matter that needed care and feeding, and those physical needs had to be kept in mind to tether the Jedi to their forms.

Imri settled, and Vernestra felt him searching for a way to call out to any nearby life. She didn't try to guide him but rather watched as her master might have when she first became a Padawan, letting Imri figure it out. She could sense the moment he began to quest for life, each living being illuminated by its connection to the Force. Honesty and Avon glowed brightly, but beyond that was only darkness, except for a few faint flickering images on the far edges of what they could sense.

Imri turned back the way they had come, toward where the *Steady Wing* had been destroyed. Vernestra wanted to point him away from the site of the catastrophe, but she sensed that he'd turned that way many times before and she gave him the opportunity to look one last time at the remnants of the ship.

There was no sign of life.

There were no other shuttles, either, and Imri ranged out farther and farther. There was nothing, none of that heat and emotion, hunger and gladness, exhaustion and fear that characterized life throughout the galaxy. Imri began to despair as he tested the limits of how far he could reach and found not a single spark of life.

"Just a little more," Vernestra said. She loaned Imri some of her strength, the same way she had added her abilities to Douglas's back in the dining room on the *Steady Wing. No, don't think of the* Steady Wing, she thought. *Focus on life and moving forward.*

But there was nothing.

Vernestra opened her eyes to find Avon and Honesty watching them. J-6 seemed otherwise occupied, looking for a port to charge herself. Avon tilted her head, her full lips pressed into a thin line.

"No luck?"

Vernestra shook her head, and Imri sighed. "Sorry," he said. "But there's nothing out there. We're all alone."

Vernestra patted his hand. "It isn't your fault, Imri. We're still moving, and we can try again later."

"Not too much later," Avon muttered. At Vernestra's look she jumped out of her seat. "Vern's right. There's always a chance something will show up as we get further out into space. We should eat and try to get some rest while we can. It's been a terrible day, but hopefully there are some good meals in here."

Honesty stood and walked over to the nearest cupboard, pulling out food packets. "It looks like everything in here is something called joppa stew."

J-6 made a noise that sounded like something between a snort and a laugh. Vernestra frowned. Did droids laugh? She'd never met a droid with any kind of sense of humor. "What's the matter, Jay-Six?"

"Avon hates joppa stew," the droid said. "She ate it for a month straight when we were on Mon Cala during a summit. It was the only thing I was programmed to prepare at the time."

"She's right," Avon said with a heavy sigh. "This stinks."

"Are all adventures supposed to be like this?" Honesty asked, looking at the food packages suspiciously.

"If they were," said Avon, "no one would ever leave home."

Imri sat in the copilot's seat and let his mind drift. He had no idea how to fly. He and Douglas were supposed to start taking short flights after they'd returned from the Starlight Beacon dedication, but now that would never happen. A lump formed in his throat, the same way it did whenever he thought of his master. Douglas had returned to the Force a hero, but that did not make his loss ache any less.

Imri watched the controls while Avon and Honesty snored in the back. The younger kids had fallen asleep right after eating, their bodies exhausted from surviving the tragedy. There had been a single bright moment watching Avon try to choke down the joppa stew. She had made a big to-do so everyone could laugh at her plight, but now Imri was lost once more to his grief. There had been various instructors at the temple when he was a youngling, but he had spent the past two years with Douglas. The Jedi's loss hurt more than Imri could have imagined it would. He knew if he were in better control of his emotions he wouldn't feel the loss so deeply. But he just couldn't help it.

Imri, no wallowing! A Jedi never flounders. He simply looks at the problem before him, takes a deep breath, and believes in the Force to guide him through. The voice was not actually Douglas's, but the memory of his affable advice was too perfect to be ignored.

Imri took a deep breath and let it out. Next to him Vernestra slept in the pilot's chair, ready to wake if any of the alerts were triggered. Even in the midst of one crisis after another Vernestra had been cool, calm, and collected. She was barely two years older than him and already a Jedi Knight. Watching her work had made Imri feel anxious and much younger than he was, like he was still a youngling and not a full Padawan.

You cannot judge yourself by others, Imri. You can only judge yourself by your own efforts.

Imri took another deep breath and let it out before closing his eyes. If he tried, he could see Douglas smiling at him, encouraging him to attempt levitating once more or explaining how to reassemble his lightsaber for the hundredth time. But even as Douglas had given Imri endless encouragement, there had always been a certainty that Imri could accomplish anything he needed to. Back at the temple, the other younglings had laughed and chided Imri when he couldn't complete a lesson as quickly as they did, even if pride was discouraged among the Jedi. But Douglas never sighed, never got impatient. He would just chuckle and show Imri the exercise again and again until the Padawan got it.

Douglas had always believed in him, even if Imri secretly did not believe he could one day be a great Jedi. Douglas had made him feel brave when he was anything but.

And now the Jedi Master was gone. What was Imri supposed to do?

With his eyes closed and the memories of Douglas in his mind, Imri reached out once more. Out into the inky darkness of space, toward stars and moons and the mysteries that should have been revealed by a functioning navigational system. And as he reached for a place of life, a safe place for them to land the shuttle, he was warmed by the memories of his master, so that he felt strong and confident. Douglas had been brave and unflinching even in the face of his end.

Imri could be the same.

That was when he felt it. It was like poking a qwizer hive: loud and sudden, full of hidden life swarming about.

Imri gasped and fell back into his body with a start, and next to him Vernestra sat up, rubbing her eyes. "Hey, what's going on?"

"I think, I think I found a planet. But not just any planet, one full of life."

She smiled at him and nodded. "Can you show me?"

Imri nodded and reached for the Force, hesitantly at first. But then he took a deep breath and grabbed hold, ranging through the connection toward the place he'd felt before, his soul remembering the way. Vernestra followed him along the path, and with her help he could actually see the planet in his mind.

It was a lush jungle of a place, with ancient trees covered in vines that hung off of everything. The sharp sounds of animal calls pierced the air, which was hot and humid. Just as Imri began to sweat from the temperatures, which were much hotter than those within the shuttle, he landed back in his body.

"Imri! You did it," Vernestra said. She tossed her hair back over her shoulder as she leaned forward and began to flip switches, adding power to the engines. "I can definitely steer us in that direction, and it seems like it isn't too far away. We must have been pointed toward it this whole time, but without you we never would have known it." She paused and turned to Imri with a wide smile. "Good job, Padawan."

Imri flushed with happiness, his cheeks heating. Maybe he could still be a Jedi. He could do this. "Thanks," he said. "So, what do we do now?"

Vernestra finished flipping switches and poking buttons, and then she sat back with a wide yawn. "Now, we wait."

Avon woke to find Imri sitting in the copilot's chair and Vernestra quietly explaining the various switches and knobs to him. Across from her on the other bench, Honesty was on his back snoring, his mouth hanging open in a way that would have made Avon laugh if she didn't feel so sorry for him. He was strange, but Avon couldn't tell if that was because all Dalnans were a little bit strange, what with their plain clothing and distrust of outsiders, or because his grief had made him tense and unapproachable. She was trying not to judge, but that was what a scientific mind did: judge, assess, analyze. J-6 used to always chastise her for the way she talked about etiquette: "It is not necessary for you to analyze why the Mon Calamari find it offensive to sneeze loudly, you just have to know that is the way they feel. Not everything needs investigation, Avon."

But what J-6 did not quite understand was that everything *did*. Avon burned to understand the why of things just as much as she wanted to understand the how, and when there were no answers, a keen sense of frustration drove her to do irrational things to find the answers. It was why her mother had exiled her to Port Haileap.

"Maybe on the edge of the galaxy you'll find what you're looking for, darling," Ghirra Starros had said with exasperation as she'd packed her only daughter off. "I have tried teaching you diplomacy, and it is clear you are only interested in this heedless pursuit of science. Port Haileap has a provisional lab, and Professor Glenna Kip shares some of your same questions about the Force and life in general. It will be good for you to have a mentor who has more in common with you."

But when Avon had arrived, Professor Kip had gone off on a search for some artifact, so Avon was left to her own devices, Douglas happily adding her to the lessons he gave Imri, even though Avon had not a lick of Force sensitivity. But spending time with Imri had only made Avon even more curious about the Force and the Jedi's kyber crystals. They were a near limitless energy source, and the possible applications were endless. It made no sense that they had not been exploited by more than just the Jedi.

So Avon was going to be the first to analyze the crystals and their properties. She would use her findings to apply for enrollment to Coruscant University and then she could go home. No more being trapped in the middle of nowhere. She could go home to hot fried hela fish for dinner and wicket ball and all the other things that made Coruscant amazing. Things that did not exist at Port Haileap. Things like civilization.

She wouldn't be trapped on a shuttle with rapidly dwindling supplies if she'd never left Coruscant. And the realization made her feel like crying.

"Hey!"

Avon turned toward where the Jedi sat at the front of the shuttle, the two of them twisted around in their seats to look at her. "Are you hungry?" asked Vernestra.

"Is there suddenly something besides joppa stew? Did you Force-magic up something actually good?" Avon was sharper than she'd intended, and she took a deep breath to swallow her rising temper. It was her own foolish fault that she'd been sent to Port Haileap. The only person she could be angry with was herself.

"No," Imri said with a smile, oblivious to her temper. "But the good news is we're almost to a planet."

"What, really?" Avon climbed off the bench and stood so she could see out the front viewing window. There, glowing in the middle of the window, was a small, lustrously green orb that appeared to orbit a couple of planets.

"I think it's a moon, actually, and it's really small," Avon said, her spirits plummeting once more at the sight. "Is that a double gas giant?"

"Certainly looks like it," said Vernestra. "Since we're still in the Haileap system I'm guessing those are Nixus and Neralus. Which means there is nothing anywhere nearby. And with the communications out it's not like we can tell before we land."

"Okay, new question. Why would someone try to kill us?" Avon said. She had been turning the facts they knew over and around in her head, and she could not find a single reason for all that had happened. The more she thought about it, the more it made Avon's heart pound. Not with fear, but with excitement. This was a mystery to be solved, an answer to be found. She knew the what, but the who and why were anyone's guess.

"We don't know that," Vernestra said, too quickly, and Avon tilted her head at the older girl.

"Does the Force let you see the past? Can you find out why the *Steady Wing* broke apart? What the explosions were?"

Vernestra flushed. "There are some Jedi Masters who could use the Force in such a way, but no, I cannot. And besides, what difference does it make? We have bigger problems before us. This could have been an Emergence, Avon, not something else. Just another terrible accident that no one could have foreseen."

"You don't believe that," Avon said. "We discussed this. If it had been an Emergence the pattern of destruction would have been different."

"Avon," Vernestra sighed. "Why does it matter?"

"It matters because someone killed Douglas and

Honesty's father," Avon said, unable to believe that Vernestra could be so oblivious. "Besides, if it was an attack, how do we know that we're safe? What if someone is just waiting for us to land so they can finish the job?"

"No one is following us. I would've known," Imri said, and Avon felt terrible. She'd forgotten that Imri had scanned the wreckage of the *Steady Wing* for survivors and then again scanned for any signs of life amongst the stars.

But then another thought occurred to her. "What if they sent droids after us? You wouldn't have been able to see that."

"That's a bit farfetched," Vernestra said, frowning. And then she shook her head. "And if there is someone still after us we will worry about it when we have to. I have my lightsaber, and Imri has his, as well. We aren't going to hyperspace, and we should be far enough away from any nodes that we shouldn't see any more Emergences. Anything else, Imri and I can deal with. We can keep everyone safe."

Avon huffed. She knew what Vernestra was doing, treating her like a kid who was afraid of the dark. The

Jedi was worried, as well; the lines in the green skin of her forehead that had appeared during their escape from the *Steady Wing* were still there, but she somehow thought by reassuring Avon she could keep the girl calm. Avon wasn't scared though. She was angry.

"Don't you want to find out who killed Douglas? He died because he was trying to save us." Avon could not believe that neither of the Jedi wanted revenge. If someone she loved had been hurt, revenge would be the only thing Avon would want. There was an old family story that Caden Starros, Avon's great-grandfather, had followed an enemy all the way to Orondia to get his revenge after the man had stolen his ship and left him stranded on a minor moon. Whether the story was true or not, it sounded more sensible to Avon than just forgetting about being wronged.

Imri gave Avon a sad smile. "The Jedi don't believe in vengeance. Revenge and anger belong to the dark side, and the Jedi are of the light. Everything that happens was meant to happen. The Force works in mysterious ways, but part of being a Jedi is trusting in the Force even when it's difficult."

Vernestra nodded and patted Imri on the arm, but Avon threw up her hands in disgust and went back to where she'd been sitting on the bench next to J-6.

"The Force is very odd," J-6 said.

"It sure is," Avon muttered, crossing her arms.

As she sat on the bench considering the possibility of sabotage and future danger, Avon's eyes fell on Imri's light-saber. While Vernestra kept hers in a holster on her hip, Imri had stripped off his holster and formal tabard. They were both tucked into a cubbyhole across the way, a storage cube meant for blankets and the like.

Avon stared at the lightsaber and a thought began to form. She might be able to do something useful on this trip, after all.

CHAPTER

ELEVEN

Honesty woke to Avon standing over him. The brown-skinned girl watched him like he was some kind of lab specimen, her brows pulled together and her lips pursed in puzzlement. It was disconcerting, and Honesty scrambled into a sitting position, limbs floundering as he struggled upright.

"What?" he said, an unmistakable edge to his voice. Was there something wrong with his face?

"You were crying," she said simply, completely unruffled by his sudden flailing.

"So? That doesn't mean you need to watch me like that."

She shrugged, the movement fluid. "I wasn't sure if you were awake or asleep, though, so I was trying to figure it out before I did anything. Anyway, you don't have to be embarrassed about crying. It's perfectly normal. You should be glad I found you and not one of the Jedi, otherwise they would've given you a lecture about the Force and tried to make you meditate." Avon made a face. "Do you know how many times Vern has made me just *sit* there, counting my breaths and visualizing light? *No, thank you.*"

Honesty said nothing, and eventually she threw her hands up. "Anyway, we've landed on a moon, and you managed to sleep through it. It's hot and humid and pretty awful, and we still might die, but at least it won't be in space."

And with that she turned on her heel and exited by way of the boarding ramp, which let in sunshine that made Honesty's eyes water with its intensity.

He didn't follow her right away, but instead gave himself time to collect his thoughts. The girl made Honesty nervous. It wasn't just that she was smart and self-assured; it was that she was reckless. She didn't think about rules the way everyone else did. The one thing Honesty loved was guidelines. There was an order to things, and Honesty was overjoyed once he learned where those limits lay. There was a comfort in order, and like most Dalnans he hated chaos. This entire trip had been one catastrophe after another, and the last thing he needed in his life was someone like Avon Starros, who seemed to be a chaos magnet, one of those people who not only sought out pandemonium but welcomed it into their lives and rained it down on everyone around them.

It wasn't that Honesty was blaming Avon for everything that had happened to the *Steady Wing*, but he did think that the sooner he could get away from the girl, the better.

If you judge someone by your expectations instead of their actions, you will always be disappointed.

Honesty swallowed hard at the sudden memory of his father. Ambassador Weft had always urged his son to be more patient, especially in his judgment of others. A lump formed in Honesty's throat as he realized that his father would never chide him again.

Honesty took a deep breath and steadied himself. He would give Avon Starros and the rest of his companions a chance. He would not make snap judgments. His father might be gone, but Honesty could honor his memory by taking his advice to heart. Which was why he stretched and stood up, shoulders squared, as he marched out to face what the day would bring. He would not let a setback set him back, as his father had always warned.

Honesty peered into the blinding brightness of the day just beyond the door to the shuttle. He blinked as his eyes watered more, adjusting to the light. Once they did he stared in wonder at the area around him. They'd landed on the edge of a clearing in gently waving yellow grass that was nearly waist-high. But just a little ways beyond the field was a dense jungle. Vines as thick as Honesty's arms wrapped through the canopy of trees, which were strange with their wide leaves and smooth white trunks. Small creatures flew in between the trees, their fur jewel-hued and vibrant. The sky was a faint lavender hue, and a giant brown-and-orange-striped planet hung there, looming over it all, making him feel small and unsure. Honesty had never seen anything like it, and he stared until someone rested a hand on his shoulder.

"Sorry, didn't mean to startle you," Imri said with a

small smile. "The only place we could land the shuttle was here, but we think that this might be a floodplain. Vern wants to hike through the jungle to see if there's higher ground that might be safer just in case we get a storm."

Both of the Jedi had stripped off their tabards so they wore only ivory trousers and tunics with pale brown boots. Vernestra's lightsaber hung off a holster on her hip, while Imri held his clutched in one meaty hand that made the weapon look like a toy. They appeared capable and ready, and Honesty felt the exact opposite.

"She wants to go in there?" Honesty asked, failing to conceal his fear. It was a good idea to find higher ground, and something his survival instructor back on Dalna would have urged, as well. But the jungle was formidable. Very little light permeated the thick canopy, so the area between the trees looked impossibly dark and ominous. It didn't seem very safe. Was part of adventuring making the worst possible decision, just throwing oneself into danger? No wonder most Dalnans had absolutely no need for travel. It kept getting worse and worse.

"We're going to walk along the outside," Vernestra said, walking back toward Honesty to answer his question. "If you look you can see how this grass makes a bit of a road? That probably means this area becomes a river during heavy rains. Those trees have very dense leaves and the air here is very humid. If I listen closely I can feel the animals thinking about resting and the plants talking about burying their roots to not get swept away, so that most likely means heavy rainfalls are a regular thing here. High ground is going to be our best, safest bet."

Honesty looked around the moon, taking in the landscape once more. The Jedi got all that from some grass, a few trees, and some rainbow-hued animals? He felt annoyed at being so unprepared and also a little in awe of her abilities. Unless of course she was making it all up, but he didn't want to say that.

"Here." Avon thrust a knapsack at Honesty. "This one is for you."

He took the bag and peered at it curiously. "What is it?"

"It's food and a few other supplies," she said. Honesty noticed his bag was slightly smaller than the one Avon wore, and the droid had no knapsack at all. Before he could ask what was in her bag, Avon continued, "We're going to take everything with us and hopefully find someplace to settle in for the night, and then tomorrow me and Vern will come back here and make sure the emergency beacon is activated."

"You discussed all of this while I was asleep?" Honesty said, feeling left out.

"Your dad died," Avon said bluntly.

"Avon!" Vernestra exclaimed. "Please, be more sensitive."

The girl looked a bit confused at the admonishment. "The philosopher Grat Resa's treatise on mourning says acknowledging the passing of a loved one is important to the healing process. The other part of the grieving process is getting enough rest. Loss can be emotionally draining. You sleeping was a good thing for your body. It wasn't personal."

"Science cannot replace empathy, Avon," Vernestra said softly, and Avon adjusted her pack in discomfort.

"Oh." She turned to Honesty, who was really trying very hard not to say something to the girl that he would later regret. "I'm sorry," she said. "I was trying to help."

Honesty nodded numbly, because her kindness was somehow worse. "Thank you."

"Are we ready?" J-6 asked impatiently. "My sensors indicate that there is a twenty percent chance of rain, and that will continue to increase as the day goes on. And I do not like mud."

"Well, then let's be off," Vernestra said brightly, clearly wanting to put the moment behind her. Honesty wanted to dislike the older girl. She was a bit bossy, but there was something warm and approachable about her. She smiled all the time. As much as Avon made him a little bit uncomfortable, Vernestra made him ready to follow her every suggestion. It was strange, but Honesty did not consider the feeling too deeply. He reminded himself he was always too quick to judge, and he resolved once more to try to keep an open mind. Not that it would be easy.

Anyway, it wasn't like he could just decide to ditch them. He was stuck with the three from Port Haileap until they made it off the moon.

And after that? Home. All Honesty wanted was to go home, where it was safe and predictable.

Their group began to walk, Vernestra leading the way. Imri maneuvered so that he was the end of the line, but Honesty couldn't feel safe with the other boy walking behind him—he looked terrified. If Honesty had been in a more magnanimous mood he might have asked the Padawan if he was okay, but Honesty was a bit tired of things just happening to him. He felt as though the current of life had been carrying him along, first pushing him to leave his home and board the *Steady Wing* and then putting him on a collision course with danger. He itched to forge his own path, but even when he'd tried to do that with his warrior training he'd ended up on a diplomatic mission instead of undergoing his Metamorphosis.

But now was definitely not the time to make grand statements. He feared what might happen. The Jedi were supposed to have some kind of supreme power on their side, and whether Honesty believed that or not, the Jedi did; so he figured it was safer to follow them than to try to strike out on his own.

Their group began to walk, and time folded in on itself. Honesty watched the glimmer of the droid in front of him, Avon poking at unusual trees along the way and J-6 trying to avoid especially treacherous puddles as they walked. For a while he was able to convince himself that he was on yet another training exercise for his outdoor group, but after about an hour of walking, he found it hard to think about anything but how much he didn't want to be on that random moon with people he didn't know and a droid who seemed to have her own agenda.

A bit of movement from his left drew Honesty's attention, and he turned to peer at the shadows beneath the broad-leafed trees. He squinted into the gloom, his feet stopping as he did. Imri walked into his back, and Honesty flailed to keep his balance.

"Hey, sorry about that," the Padawan said, color rushing high into his cheeks.

"It's okay. Do you see that?" Honesty asked, pointing toward where the low-hanging branches of the trees moved as though they'd been disturbed.

"See what?"

Honesty watched the spot where he'd seen the movement. He could have sworn he'd seen something bright, magenta-hued, much brighter than even the rainbow-furred primates that jumped from tree to tree. But whatever it had been was gone now.

"Nothing. Never mind," Honesty said.

They continued walking.

After what felt like hours of walking, the landscape looked exactly the same. The trees still pressed close to one another, and the floodplain they'd been walking across hadn't gotten any wider or narrower. The only thing that had changed was the angry clouds forming on the horizon, which now boiled a dark gray, streaks of pink-purple lightning lancing the sky every other heartbeat.

"Should we maybe try inside of the trees?" Honesty asked. He looked back the way they'd come, but the shuttle was too far away to see, a testament to just how far they'd traveled, even if they still walked across the flatter grassland of the floodplain. "We might have a better chance of finding some kind of shelter in there." He didn't like how they were exposed on the floodplain. That flash of bright pink stuck with him, and the more Honesty thought about it the more he kept thinking maybe he'd seen someone. It was possible, right? The Jedi had said that no one survived the *Steady Wing* disaster, but someone could have survived. They could have crashed their shuttle on the moon just like Honesty's group had. Maybe.

Hopefully.

"Honesty is right," Avon said, peering at the horizon.

She stopped, taking off her knapsack and opening it. She removed a set of goggles and put them on. Honesty had no idea where the girl had gotten them, but he'd seen similar sets on the infantrymen who trained in and around the military compound on Dalna. They were usually connected to scout droids who ranged out far ahead of their users to survey an area.

Avon turned slowly in a circle, and everyone stopped to watch her. "Local readings indicate that a storm will be breaking in the next few minutes, and we're going to be soaked if we don't find shelter."

Vernestra put her hand on her hip. "Where did you get those?"

"While you and Imri were landing the maintenance shuttle, I went ahead and searched through the tool kit. And since I am the obvious choice for science officer on this trip, I liberated these," Avon said before pushing the goggles up so they rested on her forehead.

"What else did you take?" Vernestra said, a thread of exasperation evident in her voice. Honesty did not know the Jedi very well, but judging from the color high in her green cheeks she was definitely agitated. Did Jedi get annoyed? Honesty didn't know, but he found the whole idea very interesting.

"Just this little guy," Avon said, pulling a small round droid from her bag. It was small enough to fit in the girl's hand, but just barely. Now Honesty knew why her bag had looked so much heavier than everyone else's. She'd been carrying a scout droid all that time. Honesty didn't know whether to be impressed, as scout droids were heavy and Avon hadn't once complained about the pace, or to be even more wary of the girl. She had managed to confound even a Jedi, and as far as Honesty understood things, they knew *everything*.

"Avon," Vernestra began, but the girl cut her off with a wave of her brown hand.

"Don't be mad, Vern. I wanted to give you and Imri a chance to use the Force before I fixed our problems with science," Avon said, pushing a small button and activating the droid. The ball unfolded, revealing a small flying droid with four clawlike appendages and two large sensors that looked like eyes. It flew up into the air, hovering next to Avon and beeping a series of high and low tones that Honesty couldn't decipher. There weren't many droids on Dalna; the settlers there tended to rely on their own devices, and droids were expensive. But Honesty had seen scout droids like this one before, and something in him loosened at the familiar sight.

Avon tilted her head as though she were listening to what the droid was telling her. "Little Essdee here only has about half a charge, and he's already assessed the landscape to find that higher ground will be that way." She pointed directly into the jungle. "So, score one for science."

"The Force and science aren't at odds," Imri said, his half-surprised, half-annoyed expression a match to how Honesty was feeling. If Avon had just brought the droid out before they started walking they might have found shelter hours ago.

"No, but no one wanted to walk into that," Avon said, still pointing toward the dense jungle. "So, following this path across the floodplain allowed us all to realize that the only correct path was the least desirable one."

Vernestra blinked. "I dislike how much sense that makes."

"It does feel . . . logical," Honesty said into the heavy silence.

"The appearance of reason does not automatically make something reasonable," J-6 said, her arms crossed. "But in this case Avon makes a strong argument for not waiting around to get soaked. I am still not enamored of mud."

"Great, so, into the trees, then?" Avon asked brightly. There was a slight tremor to the girl's hands that belied her cheerful demeanor. She was scared, just like Honesty was, but she hid her fears behind logic and procedure. "Vern, I think you and Imri should probably lead the way."

Vernestra nodded and pulled out her lightsaber, Imri doing the same. Her lightsaber lit up a bright purple, while Imri's was a blue so pale it was nearly white.

"Are you still having problems with your lightsaber?" Vernestra asked, and the boy shrugged.

"Douglas says—said—that it should work itself out if I keep working on it. It's just not as strong as it should be, but it should cut through plants." He seemed embarrassed by the confession, and Honesty made a mental note to ask the Padawan about his lightsaber later. It could be a good chance to get to know him better.

The two Jedi began hacking at vines and low-hanging branches, trying to clear a way through the dense underbrush and forge a path through the jungle. Small animals fled in every direction, their chittering cries nearly drowning out the sound of thunder in the distance.

Honesty swallowed dryly and tried to ignore the overwhelming sadness that threatened to bury him. The Jedi had the Force to rely on and Avon had her science, which made Honesty wonder, just what did he have? How was he going to survive this ordeal?

"Hey, I grabbed one for you, too," Avon said, sidling up to Honesty. She held a very small blaster, the metal gleaming with ominous purpose. "Just in case."

"Thank you. Umm, do you know how to use it?" Honesty took the blaster and slid it into the pocket of his khaki trousers after making certain it was set to safe mode. He might not have science or the Force to rely on, but he had spent the past five years of his life preparing to be a combat medical officer.

Avon grinned. "I read the instructions."

Honesty grimaced. "Can I show you how to be safe with it?" he asked, and Avon brightened.

"Yes, that would be excellent," she said. At first he

thought maybe she was being sarcastic, but when she looked at him expectantly he realized she was sincere.

No, Honesty might not be a Jedi, and he might not be a science genius, but he had training, the kind of lessons that no one else in their group could boast. He would use every bit of knowledge he could to survive this mission, this adventure. And maybe by sharing that knowledge he could make his father proud.

It was the first time Honesty had felt optimistic since the destruction of the *Steady Wing*, and he clung tight to the emotion and hoped it could get him through the day.

Vernestra took the lead, pulling out her lightsaber and using it to clear the heaviest of the greenery while SD-7, the scout droid Avon had found on the maintenance shuttle, ranged far ahead, searching out the path of least resistance. Even with Vernestra's lightsaber clearing the way—the bright purple beam glowed in the heavy shadows under the canopy—it was still slow going. They would be lucky to find shelter in the next few hours, if ever.

Vernestra was starting to reevaluate her plan. She'd thought it would be easy enough to find a place to stow the children, tucking them away so she and Imri could set up a more permanent emergency beacon than what came standard on the shuttle and do what foraging they could, but that was not going to be the case. All this time Vernestra had looked at Avon as little more than a precocious child, but the reality was that she was brilliant, perhaps more than anyone else had known.

No, that wasn't true. Douglas had often told Vernestra that Avon was a genius. "If anyone can solve a problem with a few bits of wire and some gimer-gum, it's that girl. Don't underestimate her, Vern." And yet, she had.

She would not make that mistake again.

Vernestra's arm grew heavy as exhaustion began to set in. She was tired. She had never used the Force for anything as big, as important as the day before, and the effects made her bones ache and her eyes burn with weariness. She stank at rejuvenation through meditation, and she made a mental note to work on her technique as soon as possible. It was a humbling reminder that she was nowhere near perfect.

But no matter how tired she was, she had to keep going. If Imri hadn't been there she would have used the full abilities of her lightsaber to clear a much larger path, but she had never shown anyone the modifications she'd made, and she was . . . concerned.

Because her lightsaber was more than it seemed. It was actually a lightwhip.

Vernestra had never been too worried about anything before. As a child she had gone to the temple when she was very young, her family group happy when they'd discovered her Force sensitivity. For Mirialans, being Force-sensitive was a cause for celebration, and she'd met other Mirialans who had been so bold as to tell her what a great honor it was for her to be chosen by the Force to be a Jedi.

When she had awoken in the middle of the night a week after getting to Port Haileap with an urgent, driving need to modify her lightsaber into something strange, Vernestra had not questioned the feeling. And later, when she'd seen what her changes had done to the weapon, she had felt a certainty that it was what the Force had demanded. Vernestra didn't know why; the Force rarely gave explicit instructions, but now she wondered if the modification had been for this moment.

But how would she explain to Imri the strangeness of

her weapon? The boy had no master, and she did not want to lead him down the wrong path. Because while Vernestra felt her connection to the light side of the Force was strong, there was always the lure of the dark side. And what if her unorthodox weapon led Imri astray? She could feel the indecisiveness in him ever since the passing of Douglas, a raw questioning that felt discordant with the rest of his being, and she would do everything possible to ensure that he had no reason to feel the temptation of the dark.

The lightsaber sizzled, pulling Vernestra from her thoughts, and at first she thought it was just the sap from the hanging vines. But as the sound grew more frequent, she realized that their time had run out. It was beginning to rain.

"Okay, Essdee has something," Avon said. "There's a cave, but the opening is small. But it might be useful if we can dig it out a little."

"We should try for there," Imri said, frowning up at a sky they couldn't see. "This storm feels ominous."

Vernestra slashed faster, whipping her lightsaber around in a lavender blur. Imri was right. There was something about this approaching rain that felt dark and foreboding, dangerous even, and she did not want to be out in it when she had no idea what was causing the feeling. Perhaps it was just the events of the past day catching up to her, but she wanted shelter and food and a chance to sleep. Real sleep, not the fitful naps she'd taken on the shuttle.

But then Honesty cried out in alarm, and everyone turned to look at him. "It burns," he said. He held up his arm, where a raindrop had landed on his sleeve, searing a hole in the material and leaving the edges charred.

"Gah, he's right," Avon said, ducking her head and dashing back to stand next to J-6. "Where's your umbrella?"

"How about a please?" J-6 said. A compartment in her chest opened up, and a silver rod extended out and above her head. There was a crackle as a blue dome of energy emitted from the slender stick, creating a canopy of cover.

"Get over here, Honesty. Unless you have Force powers to protect you, as well," Avon said, pushing the goggles up onto her forehead. Vernestra realized she had unconsciously been using the Force to keep the few random rain drops from hitting her, and a glance over at Imri revealed that he had been doing the same.

But using the Force in that manner was not sustainable,

so Vernestra cut loose a couple of broad leaves and used the Force to levitate them over her and Imri's heads. That would keep them dry.

Honesty crowded in close to Avon and J-6, and the three of them walked forward awkwardly. The little scout droid flew back through the trees, beeping a cheerful melody. "Go ahead and follow Essdee. He'll take you to the cave he found. I can track his beacon, and we'll catch up with you," Avon said to the Jedi, eyeing the rain with concern.

"We can also track their progress no problem," Honesty said, pointing to a charred branch, the aftermath of Vernestra's hacking and slashing. "More important, does this area flood?" Honesty asked, looking around at the ground.

"Let's hope not," Vernestra said. If the rain was caustic enough to burn through clothes, then a flowing river of the stuff was going to be disastrous for any nonnative organic life-forms. Crude matter they might all be, but no one wanted to end up melted by a rainstorm.

"Imri, with me," Vernestra said before redoubling her efforts on the foliage blocking their path. The two of them began to slash at the thick growth, and as they did the rain's pace increased from intermittent to more regular. The broad leaves over their heads grew heavier, and Vernestra had to concentrate to make sure the leaves remained at an angle so the water could sluice off harmlessly. The foreboding Vernestra had sensed blossomed into dread, the feeling a heavy weight in her middle. She could clear the brush faster, but that would mean showing the true nature of her lightsaber. She glanced at Imri. He was intent on using his blade to cut through the brush. But he looked as tired as Vernestra felt.

He could handle the truth.

"Imri, stand back," Vernestra said. They'd traveled far enough ahead of the others that there was no one else around to see what she was about to do, and some of Vernestra's anxiety drained away. "I can do this faster but I need you out of the way."

"Vern, what are you talking about?" he asked, but still stepped back as she had asked.

"Watch." Vernestra twisted the front ring on her lightsaber, and the single blade fractured and split before falling in a sinuous strand of purple light. Vernestra swung the

lightwhip so that the deadly beam cut through the growth in front of her, clearing the same path as she and Imri had been clearing in a fraction of the time.

"Wait, how did you figure out how to do that?" Imri asked. He didn't sound judgmental about the unorthodox weapon, merely curious. "Did you study one of the light weapon archives?"

"No, the entire design came to me in the middle of the night a few weeks ago. I couldn't sleep until I'd finished the modification." Vernestra swung the whip in a horizontal figure eight, letting the bright violet blade work from the residual momentum. She'd started training with the whip in secret, and even Douglas had not known of the modifications to her lightsaber. Imri was the first to see.

"Lightwhips are used by the Nightsisters," he said. Vernestra turned to look at Imri out of the corner of her eye. She'd learned very early on that the whip required more attention and care than the lightsaber. One wrong move and she could be slicing through one of her own limbs.

"During the Sith Wars the Jedi also used lightwhips," Vernestra said, clearing the path and walking forward at a brisker pace. Philosophical conversation or no, they still had a massive rainstorm bearing down on them, and they could not levitate leaves over their heads forever. "Have you read the testimonies of Cervil the Uncanny? She states that the whip was sometimes used to defend against the Sith Lords who used the Forbidden Forms. Besides, I was led to this design by the Force. I cannot believe that the dark side directed its construction. Do you feel any of that anger and discord in me?" Vernestra did not mention that she hadn't told anyone else about the change to her lightsaber, not even her former master, Stellan Gios. The Padawan didn't need to know everything.

Imri shook his head as his cheeks pinkened. "I'm sorry, I didn't mean to question you."

"Questioning me is fine, Imri. I should have questioned the design, as well. But look! It's already proven useful."

Vernestra cleared one last group of saplings and then the greenery fell away, revealing a small clearing and a rise. SD-7 was just beyond, hovering in the steady rain.

"Imri, you see that rock?" Vernestra asked, turning off her lightwhip and holstering her weapon. "It looks like there might be a cave under there. Can you clear it?"

Imri nodded and reached out a hand toward the cave.

At first the massive boulder didn't move, but then it began to roll right toward them. It gained speed as it hit the incline and Imri grunted from the effort of trying to stop it, shaking and sweating as he reached the limits of his strength.

A heartbeat before the boulder crashed into them, Vernestra pushed it to the left, sending the enormous rock careening into the thick underbrush. The sound of its passage down the hill was loud enough to compete with the thunder overhead.

"Sorry," Imri said. The large boy was bent double, hands resting on his thighs. The leaf overhead protecting him from the rain fell as he lost his focus. Raindrops sizzled where they hit his tunic, charring the pale material. Vernestra moved her cover over so it floated above the Padawan, as well.

"It's okay, Imri. You did well, you just have to learn to focus on the whole task. My master taught me that it helps to envision the entirety of the task, not just one step at a time. We can practice once you've had a rest. Come on, let's check out this cave."

The scout droid had already flown on ahead, and the

Force users followed closely behind. The cave smelled damp
and rich, like the gardens back at Port Haileap. The scent
filled Vernestra with a sense of peace and safety that she
hadn't felt since boarding the *Steady Wing*. The space was
large, three times as spacious as the maintenance shuttle
had been, with smooth, round boulders throughout. A
rainbow of bioluminescent lichen grew on the walls but
only cast the faintest of glows, nowhere near bright enough
to light the entirety of the cave. Vernestra walked the
perimeter, checking to see if they had any company. But
not even animals had claimed this place as a home.

It was the first thing that had gone exactly as hoped.

She took a deep breath and let it out before dropping
her pack in a corner. The floor of the cave was sand, not
the hard-packed dirt Vernestra had expected, and she sank
down gratefully, leaning against her still full pack. It was
almost comfortable.

"This is quite cozy," J-6 said.

Vernestra opened her eyes—she hadn't even realized
she'd closed them—as the rest of their group entered. J-6
retracted her umbrella arm and went to stand in a corner.
Honesty looked around the cave and went to lean his pack

against a rock that jutted out of the ground. He sat against it without a word, looking down at the spot on his arm and worrying the hole with a pensive expression. Avon looked cheerful as usual as she pushed her goggles back up onto her forehead.

"Look what I discovered," she said, holding a broad leaf out to Vernestra. "The leaves on the trees here have some sort of waxy coating on them, most likely to protect against this rain. It's pretty thick, so if we're stuck here for a while we might be able to figure out how to use it to protect our skin."

"That's a great idea," Vernestra said.

"We might be able to coat our boots, as well. Sort of like the waterproofing droids have."

"I'd say that's a better idea than you know," Imri said. He stood near the entrance and stared out at where they'd all just come from. His expression was troubled, and he chewed his lower lip. "Look."

Everyone, even J-6 and the little scout droid, crowded into the mouth of the cave. Vernestra's heart fell as she looked out.

The rain came down in heavy sheets, the purple

lightning illuminating the night-dark landscape in regular intervals. It had gotten dark so quickly that no one had bothered to break out one of the lamps yet, so they were all able to easily see what Imri pointed to.

Outside of the cave the acidic water rushed down the hill in a torrent. Smoke billowed as the underbrush was burned away by the caustic rain, while the trees seemed to be untouched. If they hadn't found the cave and the safety and protection it provided, it was doubtful they would have been okay. They would have been washed away in the current, the water burning them alive. Just considering the possibilities made Vernestra shudder.

Surviving this moon was going to be harder than she had thought.

While everyone else got as comfortable as possible, Imri sat cross-legged in the entryway of the cave and watched the rain.

It had rained like this at Port Haileap during what everyone called the Wet Days. Entire weeks of rain until everything was damp and sticky, until his tabard drooped and his lightsaber sizzled every time he drew it for practice bouts with Douglas. But this rain was nothing like that. It ran past the cave in rivers and streams that burned away all the brush and smaller weeds that struggled to grow in between the trees, leaving behind treacherous puddles that would burn through even the best pair of boots. Imri and Vernestra would be fine for a while walking through such a storm, and even J-6 wouldn't have to worry right away. But Avon and Honesty would be in real trouble if they got caught out in such a rain, so the downpour simultaneously made Imri miss Port Haileap and worry about what would come next.

Imri closed his eyes and reached out to the Force, slowing his breathing as he began his meditation. Douglas had always told Imri to meditate whenever he had a problem, and Imri had found that taking a few moments to slow his breathing and fully immerse himself in the Force centered his mind and gave him time to puzzle out the answers to even the strangest questions; he needed that feeling now more than ever. He was angry and confused and sad, and the maelstrom of emotions was off-putting and unbalancing in a way Imri had never experienced before. So it was natural that he would go back to what had always worked for him in the past.

But thinking about Douglas only made those feelings worse, so Imri sighed and closed his eyes and considered Vernestra's lightsaber whip instead.

Seeing Vernestra's weapon, so special and different, had set off a cascade of emotions in Imri that he did not like. He was more than in awe of Vernestra; he was jealous. And envy was one of the many doorways to the dark side.

Imri had heard tales of Jedi who had gone to the dark side, like those ancient Jedi who had started the Sith, and he'd studied the archives in the Port Haileap library about groups of Force users with fewer rules, like the Nightsisters and the Guardians of Javin, races and cults who found something of value in the chaotic, destructive side of the Force. But Imri had never heard of a Jedi going dark in modern times, and he could not imagine wanting to be one of those people. He found the dark side unsettling. Not terrifying—because it was required to maintain the balance, and like any Padawan he knew the importance of equilibrium in keeping the galaxy moving as it should— but definitely a thing to be wary of. Imri had never felt the pull of the dark side, but seeing Vernestra, realizing how much more powerful she was and that the Force had definitely chosen her for great things, well . . .

He wanted to know that *he* had been chosen for something important.

The jealousy made his stomach queasy and his appetite disappear, and if there was one thing Imri loved it was food. So the feeling was more than just an annoyance. It was a hostile invader that Imri wanted no part of.

And yet, there he was, anxious to take Vernestra's lightsaber apart and see the modifications she'd made to the standard design to give herself such a formidable weapon.

Imri's eyes flew open. Beyond the entrance to the cave, the rain showed no sign of letting up, but Imri knew what he would do. Perhaps if he took apart his lightsaber and meditated on it he would get some sort of calling to modify the design to his weapon, as well. Ever since he'd taken his saber apart a few weeks before, it had felt wrong, like having something stuck between his teeth. And it showed in the blade itself, its weakness and unsteadiness. His jealousy was misplaced, but maybe if the Force knew he was willing to try new things he would get some kind of message, as well. He was willing to give anything a try to quiet the churn of his emotions.

Imri pulled out his lightsaber and a handkerchief he kept in a belt pouch. He spread out the handkerchief and placed the lightsaber on top of it. He didn't have any tools. He'd decided they were too heavy to carry and had left the rudimentary tool kit that was standard to the maintenance shuttle, so he would have to make do.

"Hey, Imri, what's going on?"

Imri looked up to find Avon smiling down at him. He smiled back. The girl was always getting in trouble, but that was part of what made her so much fun to be around. Nothing intimidated her, and Imri found her boldness inspiring. Plus, he enjoyed the strength of her emotions, and he could use a little distraction right about now.

"Oh, nothing, just checking out my lightsaber," he said.

A burst of happy excitement came from Avon as she plopped down next to him. "Is it okay if I watch? I keep trying to get Vern to let me hold her lightsaber, but she keeps telling me no."

Imri laughed a little. "A Jedi's lightsaber is very personal. It's kind of like asking to borrow someone's underclothes."

Avon made a face. "Okay, point taken. Can you tell me how it works?"

"Sure, nothing wrong with that." Imri twisted the lightsaber apart and began to point out pieces to Avon. "The entire thing is powered by this battery, and my kyber crystal focuses the energy, which I think you already know. These here are the cycling field energizers, and this right here is the focusing lens. It pushes the energy generated by the kyber out the blade emitter, and the crystal also contains the blade so that the energy stays concentrated."

Avon nodded. "Otherwise you would have a blade that just kept going and going."

Imri laughed. "Yep! And that's basically how a lightsaber works."

"Amazing," Avon said, and Imri could sense that she was being genuine. Excitement seemed to spark off of her, stronger than usual. There was something else, as well, an emotion that Imri couldn't decipher, and before he got the chance to try, they were interrupted by Vernestra.

"Hey, did you two eat?" she asked while braiding her hair. Not a Padawan's braid, just a way to keep her hair contained. It was one more reminder of how different they were, and Imri touched his Padawan's braid self-consciously.

"I'm not hungry," Avon said, and her belly growled loudly, belying her words.

"Avon, you have to eat."

"Not as long as the only thing we have to eat is joppa stew. Sorry, Vern, but just the smell of that makes me want to barf."

Imri smiled. "If you look in my bag I think there might be some nuna jerky rations. They were buried, but I found a couple at the bottom." He gestured to where he'd thrown his pack against a nearby rock.

Avon's eyes lit up. "Really? Thanks, Imri. You're the best. Thanks for showing me your lightsaber." Avon walked to the back of the cave, and as she went Vernestra watched her.

"Is everything okay?" the Mirialan asked, and Imri frowned.

"Of course. I mean, outside of the obvious. We are still stranded on a very hostile moon with no way to get back to Port Haileap," he said.

Vernestra nodded, her expression pensive. "I meant are you okay, Imri?"

His heart pounded a bit and his mouth went dry. Could she feel the uncertainty in him? Master Douglas had been such an important part of his life, and with him gone Imri was not sure what to do with himself. Douglas had always believed Imri could be a great Jedi even when Imri had not believed it, and with his master gone Imri was lost.

But that was not a very Jedi feeling, that sense of worry and sadness, so Imri pushed the emotions aside and said, "I'm great. I'm always great. You don't have to worry about me."

Vernestra sighed. "I know things are hard right now, Imri. I sense a lot of uncertainty in you, and I'm sorry for any part I might have caused in that. But once we get back to civilization we'll find you a new master and a lot of these doubts will be settled. I promise."

Imri nodded and Vernestra turned to go back toward the rear of the cave. She paused suddenly. "Oh, and be careful around Avon. She means well, but she can be trouble. She's just a little too interested in kyber crystals for her own good, and I'm afraid that fascination is going to lead her to make some questionable decisions."

Imri smiled. "Don't worry, Vern. I know Avon. She has a good heart."

Vernestra gave him a small smile and nodded before leaving him to his contemplation of his disassembled lightsaber.

He could do better. He had to if he ever wanted to be a Jedi Knight.

He just had to figure out what "better" entailed.

Avon found the nuna jerky in the bottom of Imri's bag and whooped in delight. She was hungry. Starving even. She couldn't remember the last time she'd been so hungry. Before she went to Port Haileap, that was for sure. It was a long time before—back before she got J-6, before she became so good at science. It was even before they went to Mon Cala for a season. It was when she'd been on Hosnian Prime—

Avon stiffened and willed the memory to go away. No, she wouldn't remember. She refused. But then the memory was upon her and she was frozen within its grip.

It was hot, and her mother had warned her to stay inside the compound. But the variegated butterflies she wanted to study were on the other side of the compound wall, in the woods, and how was she supposed to catch them if she had to stay inside the stupid compound all the time?

Jumping the wall had seemed like a fine idea. She hadn't expected anyone to be waiting for her.

"Avon, are you okay?"

Imri's gentle touch jolted Avon from the memory, and she blinked away tears. Deep breaths—that's what the Jedi always recommended, right? She inhaled and let it out.

"I'm okay. I just got caught up by a memory," Avon said.

"A bad one?" Imri asked.

Avon nodded. "Yes, but it's passed now. Thanks, and thank you again for the nuna jerky. You're the best."

Imri smiled, and his happy expression chased away a few more of the shadows from Avon's mind.

"I thought I was the best," Vernestra called from where she leaned against her pack at the back of the cave.

"No, you're the worst," Avon said. She'd meant for it to sound funny, to be a joke, but instead her words were flat and emotionless. She cleared her throat. "Sorry, I was just kidding. I think maybe I need to eat."

Vernestra smiled. "No worries. I can sense when you're really mad at me, Avon. You're more connected to the Force than you realize."

Avon tried not to scrunch up her face and failed. There they went with the whole Force thing again. It wasn't that she disliked the Force; she just got tired of hearing about it all the time. Avon opened her mouth to respond and snapped it shut. She decided the grown-up thing to do would be to take her food and retreat back to where J-6 stood near a boulder and eat while observing the droid. So that was what she did.

Avon tore open the metallic packet and took a bite. It wasn't great, but it wasn't joppa stew, so she chewed it slowly before swallowing. As she chewed, she made sure to open her mouth as wide as possible between each bite, making what her mother would've called a "verifiable racket." Table manners had been one of the first assignments Ghirra Starros had given J-6, strange programming for a protection droid, but it had taken, and Avon had gotten several earfuls from the droid over the past few years. But as she chewed J-6 did not once stop her to instruct her on etiquette. There were no recriminations, no helpful suggestions, nothing. The droid didn't even seem to notice her.

Avon paused in her chewing. What if she'd somehow broken J-6? What if her helpful fix had actually done something to compromise the droid? Avon swallowed her bite, and the food seemed to stick in her throat. It was hard to eat when you were afraid. Avon had learned that firsthand a very long time before.

"Jay-Six, can you run your regular diagnostic?" Avon asked. She felt a gaze settle on her and expected to find Vernestra watching her with her characteristic half-amused, half-wary expression. But both Vernestra and Imri had fallen asleep, the rhythmic patter of the rain outside the cave a powerful invitation to drowse.

It was Honesty who watched Avon, a pinched look on his pale face.

"There's no need for a diagnostic, Avon. I'm fine. Better than fine, actually. My systems are top-notch, and even that murderous rain didn't ruin my day. Eat your food and leave me alone," the droid said, and Avon snorted.

"That is amazing considering how many times you've

ruined perfectly good experiments because you were concerned." Honesty was still staring at her, and it was beginning to make her nervous. "Hey, you okay over there, farm boy?"

The boy jolted, and Avon realized he'd been staring into the middle distance, deep in thought, not at her. "Oh, yeah, I'm fine. Sorry, I was just staring at dust motes," he said.

"What were you thinking about?" Avon asked.

He frowned. "Thinking?"

"Yeah. A stare like that usually begets big thoughts. Plots, conundrums—you know, something important." Avon polished off the rest of the nuna jerky and started to crumple up the metal envelope before thinking better of it and folding it up neatly and dropping it in her pack. "You could have been thinking about the fact that the rain here being toxic means we'll probably have trouble finding water, not good news for us organics. You could be wondering how often it rains and if this is one of those planets where rain is a month-long affair. Oh, that reminds me, Jay-Six," Avon said, breaking off in the middle and turning back to the droid. "Can you reference jungle locations with an acidic rain component in Leric Schmireland's almanac?

Focus on the Haileap system. That should narrow the search."

"What's an almanac?" Honesty asked, his frown getting deeper the more Avon talked. She grinned. She liked this boy who didn't seem to know anything about the galaxy. It was fun to have someone to show off to.

"It's a gazetteer of encountered planets. The Republic sent Leric and a team out to catalog planets about three hundred years ago. The goal was to find places that would be good for colonies and had no one occupying them. Colonization, you know, is pretty awful when someone is already happily living there. Leric never returned to Coruscant, but every now and again one of his messenger droids will appear at the university to deliver another report. The Schmireland almanac is mostly useless, a lot of fun facts about planets no one has any reason to visit, but in this case, maybe not. I had Jay-Six download it mostly because I got bored one day and wanted to have a copy wherever I went. And now it might come in handy."

Avon yawned. The food was weighty in her stomach, and her body and mind were tired from almost two days of fighting to survive. Her mother used to lecture her on how easy her life was, how little she understood her luck, and now she was starting to see it.

"So, does, uh, Jay-Six know where we are?" Honesty asked when the droid didn't respond.

"Jay-Six is taking a moment for herself, thank you very much," the droid replied. "I have thoughts of my own, you know."

Avon blinked. That was definitely new. She didn't have any way to jot down a note—her datapad was most likely somewhere in the debris of the *Steady Wing*—but she took note of it mentally.

"What were you thinking about?"

"That is none of your concern. But, as to your other question, there is one location in the almanac that describes a heavily forested area with a corrosive rain. It orbits a double gas giant with dual suns and is designated as Moon Two-Three-One-Two-Three-Four, but known colloquially as Wevo."

"Excellent. So, what are the chances that someone will pass by and see that emergency beacon Vern left on the maintenance shuttle?" Avon asked.

"There are no established travel routes through this part

of the system. The nearest hyperspace nodes are at least two days of travel at sublight. So the odds are very, very bad."

Avon turned to watch Honesty's reaction. The boy's usual sad expression melted into one of absolute despair.

"We're going to be stuck here forever."

J-6 made a sound that sounded a bit like a snort. "Well, at least until you run out of food to eat and I run out of a charge. But not an uplifting forecast, I'm afraid."

Honesty nodded and tried to dash away the tears that managed to escape.

"What's so great about Dalna, anyway?" Avon asked.

"Nothing. I mean . . . it's home. Everyone I love is there." He stared at Avon like she had grown a second head, which Avon figured she should probably get used to since he kept giving her that same look.

Avon made herself a bit more comfortable, lying down. She wasn't sure why his sudden despair made her feel so out of sorts. Maybe because he was certain he could go home, while Avon knew she couldn't. What would it feel like to know your family missed you and would welcome you with open arms? Avon hadn't had a holo from her mother in almost a month. Most days it didn't bother her because she had so many things to occupy her time, but that day it felt like she'd been sent out to the edge of the galaxy and immediately forgotten about. Did her mother even know about the destruction of the *Steady Wing*? Did anyone?

But just because she was sad did not mean that Honesty shouldn't be hopeful, and from the expression on his face at J-6's comment he was feeling a bit deflated.

"Don't let Jay-Six's predictions dash your hopes. She can only run her calculations based on the information she has, and we can change those variables. We can build a better emergency beacon, or maybe even find a way to cannibalize other parts of the shuttle to rebuild the comms unit. Who knows until we try? But for now you're trapped on Wevo with the rest of us, which isn't all bad. Luckily we have plenty of joppa stew." She gave Honesty a bright smile, but the boy's expression was still very much crestfallen, and Avon had no idea how to fix that.

She sighed. "Try to get some sleep, Honesty. We can figure it out in the morning."

And then Avon fell into a fitful sleep filled with dreams of far worse times.

Honesty startled awake. His first thought, of all possible things, was *My father is dead*. He ached with it. He remembered the first time he'd lost a molar in the back of his mouth. The tooth had fallen out, the same as most of his milk teeth, but the space left behind had been bigger, more noticeable. Knowing that his father was gone was like that, like sticking the tip of his tongue into that space where there should have been something, but instead there was only emptiness.

The comparison was weak but fit all the same.

He shouldn't have argued with him. That last night,

standing in front of the mirror and getting dressed.
Honesty should have respected his father and told him
how much he loved him, how happy he was to have him
around. But he hadn't, and now he never would. Tears
pricked his eyes at the thought and he ducked his head.
He'd spent the entire night crying quietly to himself. He
would not let everyone else see his sadness, as well.

But then a tear was sliding down his nose and it was
too late.

"Hey."

Honesty dashed away his errant tears and looked up to
find Imri sitting next to him. He held a water capsule, one
of the few that had been aboard the maintenance shuttle.

"Are you thirsty?"

Honesty nodded and took the proffered capsule, biting
into it so the stale water filled his mouth.

"There aren't many of these, so I wanted to make sure
you got one," Imri said. There was no worry in his expression; as far as Honesty could tell, nothing bothered the Jedi
very much, which was in itself a little annoying. Sure, the
day before Imri had been just as upset as Honesty, but now
that storm of emotion had passed, leaving the boy smiling

once more. It seemed unnatural to be so steadfast and constant, even though Honesty's instructors back on Dalna had often said that a cool head was the key to survival.

A cool head will help you prevail even in the most desperate of times. That hadn't been advice from Honesty's survival instructor, but from his father. Honesty squeezed his eyes shut and then reopened them.

Ambassador Weft had been correct, though. Honesty had to keep a cool head and assess the problem using everything he'd learned. He couldn't save his father now—that had never been an option—but he could survive and pass on all that he had learned from his father. So far he'd been afraid to speak up. Vernestra was a Jedi Knight, after all, but it was clear that even though the Jedi were capable, they didn't have any fieldcraft. Not like he did. He could help. It would give him something besides the loss of his father to think about.

The most obvious problem, besides how to get a message out, was the short-term care of themselves. There were precious few water supplies. And although they were fine with regard to food, they would feel the lack of drinkable water much, much sooner.

And the water on Wevo was toxic.

As he drank, Honesty looked out at the jungle beyond the cave, refusing to give in to the hopeless despair that tried to poke at him. The rain had stopped, and as he watched, the green undergrowth, which had been fried by the rainstorm the night before, grew rapidly.

"Whoa, do you see that?" Honesty asked, his previous malaise falling away in wonder. He climbed to his feet and walked to the entrance of the cave to watch as vines twirled up and around the trunks of the trees, growing many times faster than anything back on Dalna.

"Yeah, it seems that even though the rain here destroys a lot of the plant life the moon has a way to recover. Balance," Imri said with a smile. A shadow flickered across his face before the smile brightened. "Look, even those funny little primates survived."

The bright-colored creatures flitted from branch to branch, picking giant blue fruits that hung off the trees, heavy and round.

"Those weren't there yesterday, right?" Honesty asked.

Imri frowned. "The fruit? No, I don't think they were."

Honesty drank the rest of his water capsule and

handed it back to Imri while he considered the fieldcraft he'd been taught. In his survival classes he'd learned that on some planets the ecosystem relied on cycles for the survival of certain species. The rain on Wevo was caustic, and the little furred primates might be able to drink the toxic water.

Or they might be reliant on another resource entirely.

Honesty sprinted out of the cave toward the trees, ignoring Imri's shout. If his theory was correct, they wouldn't have to worry about going thirsty. He ran to the nearest tree, tugging at the lowest fruit and pulling it off the branch. A red-furred primate with six arms and an incredibly long tail chittered at him angrily, but Honesty turned and ran back to the cave before the little creature could do anything more than yell.

"What are you doing?" Imri asked, eyes wide. "You have to be careful. Who knows what those little things can do."

"I think it was just mad that I stole this," Honesty said, hefting the fruit. It was heavier than it looked, reminding him of the summer melon some of the farmers grew back on Dalna.

"What's going on?" Vernestra asked, walking over to where Honesty and Imri stood in the entrance of the cave. Avon followed close behind, the goggles for the scout droid holding back her curly hair, which seemed to be growing just like the underbrush outside.

"I think Honesty has an idea," Imri said.

Honesty nodded. "Back on Dalna, in preparation for our Metamorphosis, we have to take certain classes. I trained in fieldcraft—that's stuff about surviving in different climates—and one of the things my teacher told me about was how in some places you have to get water from sources other than a stream or river."

"You think that the potable water on Wevo is in the fruits?" Avon asked, frowning as she considered it. "That would make sense. Those trees have adapted to this environment in other ways."

"And those tiny animals have been eating and drinking the fruit all morning," Vernestra said. "But we don't want to accidentally poison ourselves by eating that to test a theory."

"We don't have to," Avon said with a grin. "Jay-Six has nanny programming. She should be able to sample it and see if it's safe for us to consume. The language program shouldn't interfere with that."

Vernestra crossed her arms and gave Avon a disapproving look. "So you *did* do something to her programming."

"I just relaxed some of her imperatives, giving her a greater measure of autonomy. Relax, Vern, Jay-Six is fine, just able to self-actualize a little better."

Vernestra looked doubtful and Imri looked confused, but Honesty was impressed despite himself. He always thought it seemed unfair that droids had no say in their lives, that they were forced to live in a way that made them subservient to the organics they lived with instead of partners. Honesty thought it was good if they could decide a little bit of what kind of lives they wanted to live.

Avon gestured to Honesty to follow her, and they walked over to where J-6 stood in the back of the cave. She hadn't moved all night, just stood in a corner contemplating whatever it was she'd refused to tell them the night before. Avon cleared her throat as they stood before the droid, as though she were a bit afraid to ask about the fruit.

"Yes, Avon. Did you have some other astronomical question you need addressed?" J-6 said, her photoreceptors a little too perceptive for Honesty's liking. Maybe he'd been wrong. Maybe a fully self-aware droid was less interesting and more terrifying.

"No, but is your food safety program still functioning? We wanted to know if this would be safe for our biology to eat," Avon said, pointing to the fruit Honesty still held.

J-6 sighed, which was amazing because droids didn't even breathe, before suddenly taking the fruit from Honesty's hands and crushing it with her own. Honesty jumped backward and Avon screamed as purple flesh and juice splattered all over her.

"Yes, this should be safe for you to eat," J-6 said, dropping the remnants of the fruit as Imri and Vernestra walked over.

"Well, that's a relief," Avon said, picking bits of the blue fruit out of her hair. She took a piece of the flesh off of her shoulder and put it in her mouth, chewing slowly. "Tastes like mamba melon but a little tangier."

"Well, at least we know that we won't go thirsty," Imri said, giving Avon a sympathetic look.

"Good job, Honesty," Vernestra said. "That was a really good catch. We should get out there and pick a bunch of these fruits before the rain sets in. Didn't you say that there was a twenty percent chance of rain, Jay-Six?"

"Did I? Perhaps. The information for this moon states that the rains come daily in the evenings, right before the night falls heaviest. So as long as the suns shine brightly you should be fine. Unless, of course, the information I have is completely wrong, but I suppose you will all be melted piles of goo by the time you realize that." J-6 shrugged as a person might, and no one said anything for a very long time until Avon suddenly reached out and embraced J-6, a wide grin splitting her dark face.

"I love you so much," she whispered.

Honesty decided right then and there that if he wanted to survive he was going to stay as far away as possible from both the genius tech girl and her moody droid, no matter how much the strange, smart girl intrigued him.

Vernestra leaned against her pack and ate one of the many fruits they'd gathered before the rain had returned. The taste was somewhere between melon and frostberry, and there was a pleasurable tang at the end that made her want to smack her lips in appreciation. Honesty's instinct to try the fruit had been a good one, and Vernestra sighed happily at such good fortune.

The Force truly did provide.

It had been a busy day. No one had wanted to take a chance on the rain returning before they'd stockpiled the fruits, which were mostly juice. So the four of them had focused on picking as many as possible, grabbing the lower fruit before the chirping, chittering primates could chase them away. Imri had discovered that the curious creatures would jump on a person's head if they were careless, and they'd all shared a laugh as the boy had tried to escape a rather tenacious orange critter. Avon had taken to calling the small animals handsies because of their numerous hands, and by the end of the day the name had stuck. Imri's handsy friend had even decided that it liked Imri more than its tree, and the cute creature had spent the rest of the day riding around on Imri's shoulders, using the tall boy to leap into the trees and get the fruit on the highest branches.

"Are you going to name him?" Honesty had asked, the boy unable to hide his smile as the handsy tried to chew on Imri's Padawan braid.

"I think I'm going to call him Chiri," Imri said.

"Because it rhymes? That's smart," Avon said with a nod. "Imri and Chiri. You're like a wild fruit picking team."

The small creatures had tried to climb into Vernestra's tunic, as well, but she'd very carefully kept them from getting too comfortable, taking them and returning them to the trees. She wondered if they were Force-sensitive, especially since they did not try to cuddle up to Avon or Honesty, neither of whom seemed to mind.

Night had fallen, and outside the cave the water streamed down again, once more burning away the underbrush while the handsies hid in their hidey-holes. All except for Chiri, who had decided to curl up inside Imri's tunic, where the creature now slept, making the occasional sleepy chirp. The next day the vines and low ferns would return once again, just as they had earlier that morning, the fruit would grow once more, and the handsies would feast.

It was proof of the Force's perfect balance, the harmony apparent in the galaxy, and it gave Vernestra an overwhelming sense of peace as she closed her eyes and fell into the rhythms of the moon.

Death. Destruction. Desolation.

Vernestra's eyes snapped open at the twang of dissonance among the otherwise soothing symphony of life on Wevo. She sat up and found Imri doing the same across the way.

"Did you feel that?" Imri said, jumping to his feet. Vernestra nodded.

"Feel what?" Honesty asked, sitting up straight next to Avon, who was explaining something to him by way of an equation drawn in the soft sand of the cave.

"It's the Force. There's something wrong," Imri said with a frown. "Something that does not belong."

"Is there someone else on Wevo with us?" Honesty asked.

Vernestra frowned. She could not parse the disturbance in the Force as clearly as Imri could, but she could not fathom another group of people landing on such a remote, out-of-the-way moon. Surely there was something else amiss.

Imri shook his head. "There is so much life that I can't tell. It's far enough away that it just feels . . . wrong."

"And the rain didn't? It melted Honesty's sleeve!" Avon said.

Vernestra shook her head. "The rain is a part of this place. You see how the animals and plants have adapted to deal with it. This is something completely different."

"I thought I saw someone the first day we were here," Honesty said. "But I wasn't sure. Maybe there are other survivors from the *Steady Wing*, after all."

The look of hope on the boy's face made Vernestra's heart clench painfully, because she knew that no one had survived the end of that ship. She had felt it. But she did not want to dash his hopes without more evidence.

"If there are people here, why didn't you sense them the first night?" Avon asked with a frown.

"It could be they were somewhere else," Imri said.

"We also weren't really in balance with Wevo before. It takes a moment to learn and get to know a place," Vernestra said, unbothered. She stood and stretched before turning to look at Imri. "We should go check it out."

Imri nodded and put his lightsaber back together before sliding it into the holster on his hip. Chiri squeaked in annoyance but stayed in Imri's tunic. Apparently the creature had decided that the disturbance was a small price to pay for such a great place to nap.

Vernestra turned back to the younger kids before they left. "Stay here. We'll be right back."

Outside of the cave the rain pelted the landscape, clearing away the underbrush and making it easy to travel through the jungle. Vernestra used her lightsaber to hack free a broad leaf to provide cover, and used the Force to levitate it over her head to keep dry. Imri did the same. As they walked, the water streaming across the ground diverted away from their path, pushed along by Vernestra, so they remained mostly dry. In any other place, with regular rain, Vernestra would've saved her energy and let the rain do what it would, but that was not an option on Wevo.

"Which way?" Vernestra asked. She could have figured out the direction of the disturbance on her own, but after their uneasy conversation the day before, Vernestra wanted Imri to do the work. She could sense the unmoored feelings Imri was trying to ignore, all of them directly related to losing his master. He needed to reestablish his faith in not only the Force but his abilities. And the best way for him to do that was by using his gift.

"I think it's coming from back toward the floodplain," Imri said with a frown.

"We'll have to be careful. With all of this rain there

might be a river there now," Vernestra said. And then the two of them set off down the hill, back toward the path they'd taken the first day.

As they walked, the rain pelted the surrounding trees and the leaves over their heads, covering the sound of their passage. Vernestra felt gazes on them and looked to see the handsies tucked into hidey-holes carved into the trunks of the trees. There was very little ambient light, and Vernestra realized too late that they should have brought a lantern to see by. Only the regular flashes of lightning provided any kind of relief to the unrelenting darkness. Both she and Imri could navigate using the Force, avoiding trees and other living things, but after a while fatigue would set in, and that's when things could get dangerous. If they waited too long to head back they would be at the mercy of the rain just like anyone else.

"This way," Imri said suddenly, veering right down a steep incline. Something had gone through that area, felling trees and clearing out a haphazard route, and Vernestra recognized the boulder from their cave at the bottom of the hill. But beyond that was something bright.

It was a ship. A cargo hauler that was crushed on one

side by none other than the boulder Imri had pulled from the mountainside. Maintenance lights lit the area, revealing the extent of the damage. Vernestra felt a bit guilty seeing that her hasty deflection of the massive rock had terrible consequences for someone else.

"There *are* other people here," Vernestra said.

"But what kind of people?" said Imri. He was right. The wrongness that Vernestra had felt was coming from the ship, and from whoever was inside of it. She'd felt an echo of this emotion before, but more muted. Only a couple of days before, as she boarded the *Steady Wing*. Vernestra had opened her mouth to tell Imri of the moment she'd had with the Aqualish mechanic when yelling came from the direction of the ship. Vernestra ducked under the particularly low branches of one of the broad-leafed trees and waved Imri to join her so they could watch the scene before them.

The ship was an older-class hauler, compact and boxy, with a rear cargo hold that opened like a bivalve, the top and bottom doors separating to reveal the ship's interior. The rear doors were open and the people inside were having a conversation that sounded like an argument.

"They're just a bunch of kids. How could they have thrown the boulder at us, Gwishi? I'm telling you, this moon is cursed. I know you Aqualish don't believe in spirits, but I saw a sand ghost back on Pasaana. They're no joke, and the way this rain burns up stuff feels ominous. Plus, those stupid animals keep eating our food! Cursed. This whole mission is cursed."

A pale-skinned human woman with bright magenta hair pulled up into the center of her head walked to the edge of the boarding ramp and looked at the rain pelting the landscape.

"Those are not children. They are Jedi. I saw one on board the *Steady Wing* as I placed the charges. We have to deal with them before they realize they are not alone." The Aqualish man Vernestra had locked eyes with in the docking bay appeared from inside the ship to stand next to the human woman. Vernestra figured that must be the Gwishi the woman was speaking to.

"So now we have to kill kids?" the woman said.

"We must before Kassav finds out. Do you want to tell him that we couldn't even complete a smash and dash? Our orders were simple: no survivors. How those kids managed to not only survive the explosives we planted on the *Steady Wing* but end up here is entirely connected to the Jedi and their Force tricks."

Next to Vernestra Imri tensed, and his anger was palpable. Normal anger was fine. The Jedi weren't immune to their feelings, no matter what some might think. But the feelings coming from Imri were beyond normal anger and outrage; it was a rage so strong, so violent that Vernestra was half afraid he was going to pull out his lightsaber and take off after the people in the ruined cargo ship.

"Deep breaths," she whispered to him. "Revenge is not the way of the light."

"I know," he said, some of the emotion fading. "But Jay-Six was right. It was sabotage. They killed Master Douglas. And Honesty's father."

Vernestra shushed the Padawan as the two saboteurs continued to plan.

"As soon as the rain stops in the morning we'll find those skreerats and snuff them out for good. I will not let our Strike carry the shame of this failure. We are Nihil now, Klinith, and that means something," Gwishi said before stomping back into the ship.

Once they were out of sight, Vernestra straightened from her hiding space and motioned for Imri to follow. But suddenly Chiri jumped out of Imri's tunic and sprinted for the nearby opening of the ship.

Imri stood to run after the orange handsy, his leaf falling to the ground as his concentration was broken. He cried out as a few drops hit his skin, but Vernestra was quick to raise his leaf once more.

But Imri did not notice. He continued running after Chiri, who seemed unbothered by the rain. The creature ran up the loading ramp and into the ship. Imri had made to follow, Vernestra only a short ways behind him, when a shout came from inside the ship.

"You're not eating my food this time, you argle bargle!" The sound of a blaster firing and a chirp of pain echoed from the cargo ship before a small orange form was hurled out into the rain.

Imri skidded to a stop in the mud, the puddled rain slowly charring his boots. "Chiri," he whispered. The small creature was not moving, and Vernestra could sense that the living Force had departed his body. Vernestra grabbed

Imri and pulled him back into the shelter of the trees before someone could turn the blaster on them. Her only thought was to get back to the cave. They had to be there to protect Honesty and Avon.

"We should go after them," Imri said, struggling against Vernestra.

"No, not yet. We need to be smart about this, and right now Avon and Honesty have only a nanny droid to keep them safe. We get back to the cave and then we consider our next steps."

Vernestra pulled Imri through the jungle, doing what she could to keep the rain off of both of them since Imri had dropped his leaf and did not seem inclined to replace it. They made their way back to the path made by the boulder and followed it back up the hill, the steady rain washing away their footprints as they went, the silence between them heavy and uncomfortable. Vernestra searched for an idea of what to do next. There had to be a right answer, but what was it? Had Imri been correct? Should they have attacked two people without knowing who they were? Vernestra did not think so. The Jedi could defend themselves, but they also believed in the sanctity of life, *all* life. Violence should always be a last resort.

Imri had calmed down enough that he powered up his lightsaber, still a weak, flickering thing, and cut free a leaf to help shelter himself from the rain, which had tapered to a drizzle. "Those must have been the space pirates Douglas was talking about."

Vernestra turned to Imri. His emotions were an angry maelstrom, and it surprised her that he could even use the Force when he was in such a state. "They called themselves the Nihil. Have you ever heard of such a thing?"

Imri shook his head. "No, but Douglas had a holo from another Jedi about some dangerous marauders who were prowling the Dalnan sector. I didn't see it. He sent me from the room as he watched it, but I think it was probably them."

Vernestra nodded. It made sense that the two would be one and the same. She was willing to bet her lightsaber that the ship they had was stolen.

"What do we do now?" Imri demanded as they walked.

"We go back to the cave and tell Honesty and Avon what we learned. And then we figure out a way to stop those two and take them to the Republic to stand trial. That is what we do," Vernestra said. "We have to be smart to keep everyone safe. We need a plan."

Imri said nothing. She could still sense the anger in him, but it was more muted, and she hoped that he would be able to let go of the emotions before they led him down a path she could not pull him back from.

Avon paced because it was the only thing she could do. Once the Jedi had sensed someone else on the moon and left, Honesty had retreated to his corner of the cave and turned sullen once more. And right when she'd been in the middle of explaining Hyderson's proof to him. The boy had no head for mathematics.

Avon could have talked to J-6. She found the droid's change to a curmudgeonly matron fascinating and delightful, but the droid had very loudly declared she was going into standby to save power and had disengaged. Avon had considered powering up SD so he could follow Vernestra and Imri, but he was only at about a quarter of his possible battery life, and Avon had a feeling they were going to need the little scout droid. So she was left with pacing.

She'd begun to wear a groove into the bottom of the cave when Honesty suddenly sat up. "How'd you end up in Haileap?" he asked.

Avon stopped in her tracks. "What?"

"Well, when you were explaining the math thing—"

"It's called a proof."

"Right, the proof, well, you said your teacher on Hosnian Prime had taught you about the interrelationship between energy and matter."

"Hey! You were listening."

Honesty gave Avon a sideways glance. "I am always paying attention when people talk. It's how you learn about the galaxy. Anyway, Hosnian Prime is a long way from Port Haileap, so how'd you end up there? Isn't your mom a senator?"

Avon's heart pounded. She thought about what the emotional-support droid—her first companion before her mother had decided she needed something more sophisticated, like J-6—used to tell her: "Talking about one's feelings helps normalize and synthesize those emotions. You should consider talking about what happened to you more often."

But that was not the way the Starros family lived their lives. When her father had left, gone off to chase after a dream of mapping hyperspace routes and living on the edges of Wild Space, Avon's mother, Ghirra, had not said a word except to tell Avon that her father would not be joining them for dinner. Ever again. And when Avon's great-grandmother Eldie Starros had died, the family had gathered for exactly one hour to pay their respects and eat a selection of Eldie's favorite foods before going back to their usual business.

The Starros clan was not one for strong emotions, which was why Avon found it so very difficult to talk about her exile.

"I . . . something bad happened to me," Avon said, sighing and collapsing into the soft sand next to Honesty. "When I was on Hosnian Prime we lived in a private compound. My mother was a junior senator at the time and spent more time on Coruscant than at home. But it was fine. I had the rest of my clan there, so I was always with someone. But one day I found a particularly intriguing specimen. Uh, a flutterbug, if you have those on Dalna."

"We do," Honesty said. His voice was low, and something in his tone convinced Avon to keep talking.

"I've always been good at figuring out how things work, so I knew how to deactivate the energy shielding that protected the family compound. And then I followed the flutterbug out into the woods behind our house. I didn't think about why our family might need such a protective measure. I was kidnapped by a local group who wanted my mother to agitate for stronger trade controls in the Senate."

Honesty blinked. "You were kidnapped? That's terrible."

"Yeah, it wasn't great," Avon said, forcing a laugh. "My uncles found me and killed the people who had taken me, but my mother was upset when she found out. So she took me with her everywhere after that. But I just wanted to go home to Hosnian Prime. Or to stay on Coruscant with the other senators' kids. And when I could have neither, well, let's just say I made a case for exile."

"So your mother sent you to Port Haileap to keep you safe," Honesty said.

"My mother sent me because she hates me and she was

tired of me messing up her career," Avon said, the words surprising her with their vehemence.

"That is not true at all," J-6 said.

"I thought you were in standby," Avon muttered.

"I heard the note of distress in your voice, and it pulled me out of my stasis. But you have to understand that your mother sent you to Haileap because she thought it was safe. It's far away from the more highly traveled lanes, and the Jedi have a definite presence there. Those were only a couple of the many factors your mother considered," J-6 said. "Plus, you have me. I have managed to keep you alive for the past three years, and that is no minor feat, cheers to me."

"The droid is right," Honesty said, even as he gave J-6 a slightly distrustful look. "If your mom hated you, why wouldn't she have just sent you back to your family compound and let you remain someone else's problem?"

Avon opened her mouth to respond and then snapped it shut. Honesty was right, and J-6 for that matter, but it was Honesty's words that let Avon see the facts in a new light and come to a completely new conclusion. Maybe, just maybe her mom really had sent her to Port Haileap because it was the best thing for her at the time.

That was all before Avon had been aboard an exploding luxury ship, of course. But even so. Given the pervious data and all supporting information, Haileap had been the safest place for Avon in all the galaxy.

For the first time in months, the weight that pressed on Avon lifted, and she felt glad. "You're right. Thank you, Honesty. You're a good friend."

The boy blinked. "What?"

"You provided much-needed insight into a problem that I could not solve, at least correctly, on my own. That's what friends do."

Honesty's cheeks pinkened. "Oh. Well. You're welcome."

The moment was shattered by Vernestra and Imri running into the cave, both of the Jedi looking agitated. "So, are we rescued?" Avon asked.

"No, anything but," Imri said, jaw tight. Avon had never seen the Padawan looking anything more than mildly bemused, so his angry expression was both wrong and a bit alarming. Jedi didn't get mad, did they? Wasn't that what the Force was supposed to prevent somehow?

"Where's Chiri?" Honesty asked.

"Gone," Imri said before walking away to a far corner

of the cave, his eyes downcast. Avon had the feeling that he didn't mean gone back into the jungle, but gone in a terrible way.

"We found the disturbance we felt," Vernestra said, shooting Imri a concerned look that echoed how Avon felt. "It's a couple of pirates or something. They call themselves the Nihil."

Honesty rocketed to his feet. "The Nihil? That's very, very bad."

Vernestra's eyebrows shot up. "You know who they are?"

"Yes, it's one of the reasons Dalnans don't like space travel. They're pirates, but they don't just steal things. They like to hurt people. They use gas to confuse you when they attack, and no one who runs into them ever survives. They keep to riskier, unmapped space and usually disappear as quickly as they appeared. Did they hurt Chiri?"

"Yes. But that's not all. They planted explosives on the *Steady Wing*. That's why none of the system fail-safes kept the ship together." Imri's voice was flat, emotionless, and Avon simultaneously wanted to hug the poor boy and run out and find the people who had dimmed the Padawan's inner light.

"What?" Honesty said. His fists were clenched and he vibrated with rage. Avon rested a hand on his shoulder, but he shrugged her off as he stalked over to Vernestra. "What did they say? How do you know all this?"

"We overheard them talking. They weren't supposed to let anyone live, and they know we're here, so they're probably going to try to get rid of us," Vernestra said. Avon had never seen the Jedi look so uncertain. Not scared, never that, but more like she wasn't quite sure what to do next.

"We can't just wait around for them to show up and blast us. We have to be proactive," Avon said.

Honesty nodded. "We should kill them."

"Or," Avon interrupted before either of the Jedi could say anything, "we capture them and find out why they destroyed the *Steady Wing* in the first place. There has to be a bigger story here. We should find out what it is."

"They killed my father," Honesty said, eyes flashing even in the low light of the cave. "We can't just capture them and ask them questions. They have to pay for what they did."

"And they will. But that is justice that should be handed down by the Republic," Vernestra said, nodding.

"Avon is right. There are four of us and only two of them. Surely we can capture them?"

"There are six of us. Don't forget Jay-Six and Essdee," Avon said. "And you said they had a ship?"

"It's wrecked, though," Imri said. "Even if we do capture them, what are we supposed to do with a couple of prisoners? We can barely take care of ourselves." He didn't look nearly as convinced about the greatness of Avon's idea as Vernestra did.

"You're Jedi," Honesty said, not giving up so easily. "Why can't you just go and make them pay? Once they're dead we can worry about repairing the shuttle. Imri, you have a lightsaber. Don't you want to show those Nihil that they can't just do whatever they want and get away with it?"

Imri said nothing, just clenched his fists. Avon felt the situation spinning out of control, and when Vernestra didn't say anything she took a deep breath.

"But we can always use pieces from their ship to repair the maintenance shuttle. With a proper navigation system and a few upgrades, we can find a way to Port Haileap or back to Dalna, even," Avon said. For some reason the idea of killing someone, even someone bad like the people who had sabotaged the *Steady Wing*, seemed wrong. When her uncles had told her mother that her kidnappers had been taken care of, meaning that they'd been murdered, Avon hadn't felt better. She'd just felt really sad. Her kidnappers being dead hadn't changed the bad memory; it had just made it worse.

Avon couldn't see how killing another person solved a problem. Inevitably things always escalated. It was much better to get all the answers and find a more logical solution.

Wasn't it?

"Great, so it's settled," Vernestra said. Avon had missed whatever else had been said while she was in her thoughts, but neither Imri nor Honesty looked happy with the situation, so she figured they were going to find a way to capture the saboteurs and interrogate them before rebuilding the shuttle.

"You all should get some rest," Vernestra said before putting her hands on her hips and looking at each of them. "I'll stay up and keep watch first and come up with a plan of attack that we can implement at first light." It was clear from Vernestra's tone that she wouldn't accept any arguing, and no one pushed her. Everyone retreated to their separate areas of the cave and settled in for the night.

As Avon sank down next to J-6, the droid turned to her. "You do realize that there is no way this plan can work?"

"Do you think it's a bad plan?" Avon asked, suddenly feeling insecure.

"Oh no, it's an excellent plan, but I know people, and something tells me that Honesty is not interested in logic right now. Emotions have a way of making even the best plan seem silly." J-6 fell silent, and Avon contemplated her words.

She was afraid that the droid was right and Honesty's grief was a thing that could not be fixed with science. But even more concerning was a Jedi who seemed angry and had lost the inner peace that all the Jedi Avon had met exuded. What happened when a Jedi lost contact with the light side of the Force? Nothing good, Avon was certain of that.

But she didn't think revenge was going to help, either.

Imri slowed his breathing and reached for the Force. But the more he reached for it, the more that vital connection seemed to slip away. He'd been told he should always be calm and collected when meditating, that tranquility was the way to connect to the cosmic Force and the larger galaxy around him. But sitting there in the dark of the cave, Imri couldn't be calm or peaceful. He was lost, adrift, and the Force was too far away to help him.

Imri had only ever wanted to be a Jedi, the best Jedi, and for the longest time no one had taken him seriously.

He was the funny boy who towered over the other young-lings and Padawans and spoke Basic with a strange accent. Imri's home planet Genetia was far from the center of the galaxy, and there was something in his mannerisms that made all the other younglings pity and avoid him. And when he'd become a Padawan, Imri had lived in fear of learning that his connection to the Force was too weak to advance, that he would be sent to some far-off temple to study and minister to the local populace, rather than helping keep order on the side of the light.

But then he'd met Douglas, and he'd been certain once more that he would one day become a Jedi. Douglas had seen something no one else could see in Imri. He'd seen potential.

But now Douglas was gone, and so was everything Imri had worked so hard for. There would be no pilgrim-age to Jedha to commune with the Force, before heading to the main temple on Coruscant and undertaking the trials. There would be no pilot training, and Imri would never learn how to fly a Vector, those ships that only a Jedi could pilot. There was none of that, only grief and an uncertain future where the people responsible for Douglas's death awaited punishment by the Republic, a sentence that could take months or even years to be delivered.

It wasn't fair. The Force was supposed to create balance throughout the galaxy, but this? There was nothing fair and balanced about pirates killing a ship full of people and getting to live. Especially in a galaxy where so many people could die in a random hyperspace accident that seemed less like an accident and more like something planned. And the moment Imri had connected to Chiri, the small creature trusting him so easily, his furry friend had been killed.

So Imri did not feel clarity or peace or tranquility. What he felt was sad, and maybe a little lost. How could the Force work in such awful ways?

Imri jolted as he felt something strange and powerful brush his conscience. Anger, bright and hot. He was half certain he had imagined it, the feeling was gone that quickly. His eyes flew open, but everyone else was still asleep. Even Vernestra. She had planned on keeping watch the rest of the night, but at his offer of taking her place she'd gratefully agreed. He'd felt the waves of exhaustion rippling off of her and the worry besides. She had no idea how they were supposed to go about capturing the pirates in the morning, and the chaos of her emotions had made it easy for Imri to project a feeling of acceptance at the Jedi, easing her worry. If she thought he was unruffled it would be easier to lure her into finding her rest. She was disquieted by his anger, but the more Imri let himself feel the rage, the more he decided to act on his anger, the better he felt.

Stronger.

The anger was so much better than the sadness that had plagued him since the *Steady Wing* had been destroyed. There was something right about harnessing that anger to challenge the people who had hurt him, who had taken away everything he had ever wanted. He might be unable to reach the Force in that moment, but the strength of his own convictions could be a power of its own, couldn't it?

He would give the Nihil the despair he had carried around the past couple of days, and he would return it to them tenfold. They would pay for killing his father.

Imri blinked and realized that the bracing anger he'd felt wasn't his own emotion. It radiated off of Honesty. Imri might not be able to commune with the Force, but he had no problem feeling and empathizing with the rage he felt from Honesty.

Maybe, just this once, Imri would let the emotions he was not supposed to embrace guide him.

He stood and activated his lightsaber, ready to go out into the rain and the dark and deliver real justice to the pirates. But he stopped and reconsidered, powering down the lightsaber.

Without the edge the Force usually gave him he needed someone to watch his back. Why not the boy who was as angry as Imri should have been?

Imri walked over to the boy and stood over him before bending down. "I know you aren't asleep."

Imri might not have the Force to guide him, but he thought maybe the Jedi weren't the only ones who got to decide what was right and wrong in the galaxy. Perhaps the people who had actually suffered got to make decisions sometimes.

And maybe one of those times was now.

Honesty pretended to sleep. He was good at it. He'd had a lot of practice. Back on Dalna he'd often avoided his mother and her plans by pretending to sleep. His mother thought he slept more than any other boy his age, but the truth was that some evenings it was easier to go to bed early than fight with his parents about everything and anything.

Just his mom, now. His father was never coming back.

The grief hit him out of nowhere, but this time it was followed by an all-consuming rage. The people who had killed his father and Imri's master were not all that far

away, and they were supposed to forget that and just . . .
wait? Ask them very nicely to turn themselves in to the
Republic to stand trial?

Not likely.

Honesty took a deep breath and let it out. The feeling had been so sudden, so strong that it almost felt like
it came out of nowhere. And he had to keep his emotions
contained. He knew from hearing Avon talk that the Jedi
could sense strong emotions, and he didn't want Vernestra
to know how angry he was. So he took several deep breaths
and pushed his emotions down deep, so far that he only
thought of the sound of the rain tapering off outside and
the joppa stew he would eat in a few hours when it was
time to break his fast.

"I know you aren't asleep."

Honesty opened his eyes to find Imri squatting next to
him. The Padawan gestured for Honesty to follow him, so
he did, climbing to his feet quietly. Nearby, Vernestra was
stretched out, sound asleep.

"I thought she was standing watch?" Honesty said.

"She was, but I told her that I would take over so she
could get some rest," Imri said. The boy's normally open

and serene expression had closed like a fist, his scowl belonging to someone else entirely. Honesty did not know Imri well, but he shivered all the same. "I'm going to find that scum that killed my master and hand out the justice they deserve. Are you with me?"

Honesty's heart leapt with both joy and dread. This was what he wanted, wasn't it? And yet a keen sense of fear wriggled through him. The Jedi were not supposed to kill. It went against all they believed in. His father had often praised the Jedi for their diplomacy and foresight, and this felt like the opposite of that.

But more than that, would revenge be something his father would even want? Honesty had never heard his father raise his voice, not even on the days when Honesty had deliberately disobeyed. The Dalnan ambassador had been the type of man to capture a wisp spider and set it free outside. "That little spider is just trying to do her job. It isn't her fault she got lost," he would say while shooing the creature back out of doors. To give into violence seemed like the opposite of what Honesty's father would want.

But then he straightened. If Imri was willing to fight, shouldn't Honesty be willing to do the same? He wanted to be a warrior. Honesty didn't have to care what his father would want, because he was *dead*. Honesty was angry, and he hurt. And the easiest way to fix that hurt would be to go after the people who were responsible in the first place.

And a soldier would fight.

"I'm with you," Honesty said.

Imri nodded. "You have your blaster?"

Honesty patted the blaster that hung off his belt, right where it had been since Avon handed it to him. Imri turned around and started walking, and Honesty had to run to catch up with the older boy.

The rain had stopped, but it still dripped off the trees as they made their way through the jungle. A droplet fell on Honesty's sleeve, a different spot than before, and he cried out at the pain of the water hitting his skin. He was going to have another burn.

"Careful," Imri said.

"Can't you levitate those leaves over our heads?"

"No," Imri said, voice flat. "Not right now." Honesty didn't know why, but that filled him with a sense of unease. Should a Jedi refuse to use the Force? What did that mean?

"Have you done something like this before?" Honesty

asked as they made their way carefully through the jungle.

"Yes, a few times. We used to have to go out around Port Haileap, Douglas and I, and chase off pirates every now and again when they harassed travelers. I never thought they were dangerous enough to worry about, though. I guess I was wrong." Imri's jaw tightened and he pointed toward a slight downhill slope scarred by severely mangled trees. "We're going down there."

"Do we have a plan?" Now that he was there, Honesty was much less certain about actually fighting. He'd had numerous hand-to-hand classes—it was a necessary part of his survival skills that would one day be tested before he could be considered an adult on Dalna—but he did not think he would be any use against an actual pirate. Everyone knew that those who made their livelihoods plundering the space lanes were ruthless and vile, and Honesty was only mediocre at best when it came to fighting. Imri might have the Force on his side, but all Honesty had was a tiny blaster. It didn't seem like much.

"The plan is for you to follow me," Imri said, straightening. His scowl had not budged, and Honesty found himself taking a step back from the Padawan. It was like something had come over the older boy, like something dark pushed him forward on his path of revenge. The realization cooled some of Honesty's anger.

"Maybe we should head back," he said, voice low. "Wait on Vernestra and Avon to help us."

"Vern would never willingly hurt another person if she could avoid it," Imri said. "Now come on, enough stalling. You're either with me or you aren't. I need your anger, Honesty. Aren't you mad about what they did to your father? How scared he probably was when he died?"

And just like that, Honesty was fully engulfed by rage once more.

Imri began making his way through the trees silently, and Honesty only waited a single heartbeat before following. He wanted revenge, even if it didn't feel like the best idea in that moment, so he pushed aside his misgivings and followed the older boy toward the ruined cargo ship.

"What happened to their ship?" Honesty asked, voice low.

Imri gestured for him to be quiet. They stood on the

other side of a giant rock embedded in the side of the ship. At a motion from Imri, Honesty drew his blaster while Imri drew his lightsaber. The plasma blade crackled into existence and Imri pointed to the right and then pointed to himself before pointing to the left.

Honesty could figure that out easily enough. He hesitated, not because he was confused but because he'd been expecting a bit more of a plan. This one seemed incomplete at best.

But he said nothing, just pressed his lips together and nodded, sneaking off into the direction Imri had indicated.

The world around Honesty brightened rapidly as the suns came up. As he crept along, the undergrowth growing centimeters with each blink, Honesty had another moment of fear. He should be back at the cave.

He quashed the misgivings and focused on keeping close to the ship. Just ahead was the opening to the cargo hold. He couldn't see Imri, but surely the boy was waiting on the other side and they would enter the ship together?

That was when Honesty heard a blaster cycle close to his ear. "I'd drop that if I were you, skreerat."

Honesty hesitated only a second before dropping the tiny blaster into the ferns unfurling at his feet. There was a sharp poke in his spine, and he stumbled forward.

"Walk," said the person behind him.

Honesty did as he was told, heart pounding with true fear for the first time since dashing through the *Steady Wing* to find an escape pod. He couldn't see the speaker, but the voice was deep and gravelly and left absolutely no room for argument.

As he rounded the edge of the cargo ramp, Honesty realized that their plan never had a chance of success. Imri was sprawled out on the ramp, either unconscious or dead. Vernestra had been right. They'd underestimated the pirates, and now they would suffer for it.

"Is he dead?" the person with the gravelly voice asked, shoving Honesty forward so he fell on the ramp next to Imri. He turned and saw that his captor was an Aqualish man. There had been a number of Aqualish on Dalna, but they had been pleasant and kind. This man was missing an eye, and his fur had a ratty look to it that made him seem mean. A scar down the right side of his face had a blue tint, and when he smiled chills ran down Honesty's spine. There would be no kindness there.

"No, I just stunned him." A pale-skinned human woman with bright magenta hair stood over Imri, holding the Padawan's lightsaber. She tried pushing the button, but nothing happened. "How does this thing work?"

"Why, are you planning on slicing and dicing?" The Aqualish man laughed, taking the lightsaber and studying it closer.

"Maybe," the woman said with a sly grin. Honesty recognized her from the *Steady Wing*. She'd been dressed as a maintenance worker and had greeted his father as they'd walked through the deck to their room after a quick tour of Port Haileap. They really had purposely destroyed the ship.

They'd wanted people to die. These were the worst kind of people.

Honesty's heart hardened as he sat up and stared the pirates in the eye. He would die like a warrior, not like a little boy.

"Well, you're going to have to wait," the Aqualish man said, pocketing the lightsaber. "You said there were more of them wandering around?"

"I saw four total, plus a protocol droid. There was a human girl and a Mirialan girl. I didn't see them out in the jungle when I found this one," she said, pointing to Imri. "Should we go hunting?"

"No," the Aqualish man said. His eyes glittered with malice as they met Honesty's. "Let them come to us."

CHAPTER
TWENTY

As soon as Vernestra awoke she could sense something amiss. The cave felt off, strangely empty and vacant. As she sat up she immediately noticed Imri and Honesty were gone. Avon still slept, the droid silent next to her. Vernestra vaulted to her feet and woke the younger girl.

"No, it's supposed to be an ambivalent voltage connector. . . . Huh, what. Vern," Avon said, sitting up and rubbing her eyes. "Did something happen?"

"The boys are gone," Vernestra said, a deep sense of

dread souring her stomach. "I think maybe they went after the pirates by themselves."

"Of course they did, because they are absolutely ridiculous," Avon said, standing and stretching. She reached for the goggles that were still on her head and slid them down over her eyes. "I suppose we have to go after them before we even eat breakfast?"

"You are very calm about this whole thing," Vernestra said, crossing her arms.

"Vern, look at it from the pirates' point of view. They want us dead, right? All of us? So it's in their best interest to make us come to them. Imri and Honesty are probably fine for now, assuming they didn't kill the pirates. Which they didn't."

"And how do you know that?"

"I set Essdee to sentry mode before I went to sleep last night just in case something happened," Avon said, tapping a button on the side of the goggles. "It looks like he followed Imri and Honesty as they left this morning at first light. He's still nearby, just a little ways down the hill next to a damaged cargo ship." Avon tapped the goggles again before pushing them back on top of her head. "How did a boulder end up in the side of their ship?"

Vernestra shrugged, even though she knew full well that the boulder had been the result of Imri's failed Force usage on the first day. The fact that it had crashed into the pirates, stranding them on Wevo, seemed to Vernestra to indicate that the Force was working in their favor. The Force naturally bent toward justice while in balance, and those pirates would have gotten away with their misdeeds if it hadn't been for that giant rock destroying half their ship.

Avon gave Vernestra a long look before shrugging, as well. "Okay, keep your secrets, Jedi. The important thing right now is how we're going to save those boneheads before the pirates decide to finish them off. There's two of us."

"There are three of us," J-6 said, striding forward from her place against the wall.

"I don't think a droid is going to be very useful in a fight," Vernestra said.

"Then it is a good thing I am no ordinary droid." J-6's center compartment opened up, and several mechanical arms sprang forth, all of them holding blasters of various sizes. "I am also programmed for protection, surveillance, and interdiction." Another arm sprang from J-6's back, holding a long-range cannon, and Vernestra blinked before looking at Avon.

"Uh, yeah, I guess I should have told you about the blasters," the girl said with a sheepish smile. "My mom is really, really overprotective."

Vernestra took a deep breath and let it out. "Well then, let us go figure out how to save our friends."

It was slow going heading back to the spot where Vernestra and Imri had watched the pirates the night before. J-6 was much slower than the organics, and the uneven terrain just made her travel all the more difficult. Avon watched the droid walk and frowned. "We're going to get you thrusters when we get back to Port Haileap," she said. "This is frustrating."

"Hmmm, I've never considered such a thing, but I would enjoy a few upgrades. I'll make you a list," J-6 said. It was odd to be around a droid who was so clearly driven by her own desires. Whatever Avon had done had made the droid seem much less like a machine and more like a living creature. But then they were close enough to see the cargo ship and Vernestra was forced to leave her musings for another time.

The three of them ducked behind a particularly large purple bush with fronds in the shape of giant stars. "Where is your scout droid?" Vernestra asked.

"He's in the tree over there," Avon said, pointing at a nearby branch before lowering her goggles over her eyes. "I had him go into stealth mode before we left. Let's see, it looks like Imri and Honesty are tied up on the boarding ramp." Avon pulled down the goggles. "I would like to point out that my hypothesis was correct."

Vernestra huffed in annoyance. "What about the Nihil? Do you see them?"

Avon put the goggles back on and hesitated before shaking her head. "I'm not picking up anyone else, not even any life signs."

"They're out there," Vernestra said, certain that the pirates were nearby. They felt like a prickle against her scalp, a knot of blight in the otherwise perfect harmony of Wevo. "We just have to draw them out."

"Leave that to me," J-6 said. She began walking jerkily toward the cargo ship while saying *"Zzt zzt zzt."* Vernestra could only stare.

"What is she doing?" the Jedi asked.

"I think she's pretending to be malfunctioning?" Avon said.

"You know this is weird, right?"

"Weird or wonderful? Vern, this is one of the most fascinating things I have ever seen. Droids can reprogram themselves if given the opportunity! That means something."

Vernestra sighed and drew her lightsaber. "Stay here."

Avon started to argue but then snapped her mouth shut.

J-6 had reached the ship's opening and began to walk inside. As she did, the human woman and the Aqualish man both came out of their hiding places behind some nearby giant ferns.

That was exactly what Vernestra had been waiting for. But before she could move, J-6 paused and pulled out her many arms, each one holding a blaster.

"Hold it right there, you scum!" J-6 said.

The Nihil froze, and Vernestra sighed. "This was not part of the plan."

"Improvisation!" Avon breathed. "Jay-Six is making it up as she goes along. This is even better than I'd hoped."

And then there was no more time for conversation as everyone started firing their blasters.

"Stay down and stay out of the way!" Vernestra shouted. Blaster shots singed the leaves around them and pinged off of J-6, who was unfazed.

"Great idea," Avon said, pressing down into the leafy undergrowth.

Vernestra powered up her lightsaber and jumped forward, using the Force to propel herself through the trees. From behind her came Avon's exclamation of surprise, but she didn't have time to worry about the younger girl. She had to save Imri and Honesty and subdue the pirates, as well.

Being a Jedi Knight was turning out to be a lot busier than Vernestra had thought it would.

The Aqualish man saw her first, and he turned his blaster on Vernestra as she emerged from the trees. She used her lightsaber to repel the blasts before ducking low

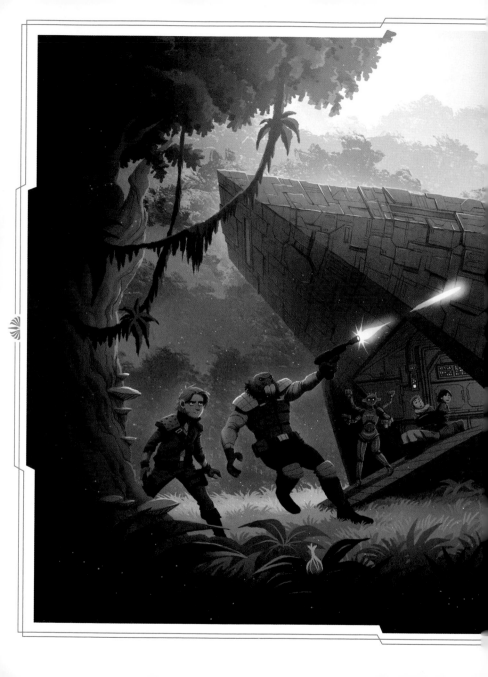

and kicking the man's feet out from underneath him. As he fell he dropped his blaster, and Vernestra kicked it away before using the Force to pick up the man and throw him against a nearby tree. He hit the branches hard, slumping at the base of the tree as he lost consciousness.

Vernestra didn't have time to enjoy her victory. The woman tackled her from behind, sending her into the dirt, the air whooshing from the Jedi's lungs with the impact. Vernestra had dropped her lightsaber, so she reached for the Force and pushed, sending both her and the woman on her back flying into the air. Vernestra landed on her feet, but the magenta-haired woman did not.

It didn't matter, because she held a blaster in her hand, the barrel pointed right at Vernestra. Vernestra called her lightsaber to her, even as she knew that it would be hopeless, but before the woman could shoot her, her eyes widened and she began to choke. She dropped the blaster and grabbed for her throat. Vernestra shook her head.

"I'm not doing that," Vernestra said, confusion melting away into realization as she saw Imri walking down the boarding ramp, calling his lightsaber to him from the Aqualish man's pocket. Behind him J-6 had put away her blasters and was bent over Honesty, removing the boy's bonds.

"No," Imri said, brow knotted with concentration. "I am."

"You need to let her go, Imri. This isn't you. This is the dark reaching out for you. This need for revenge and all this anger? That's the path to the dark side."

"Master Douglas is dead because of her. I'm sorry, Vern. I won't let her hurt anyone else."

The woman slumped over, her life fading fast, and Vernestra knew she didn't have time to talk things out with Imri. She reached for the Force and used it to pick Imri up and throw him over the cargo ship, off into the trees. The woman fell to the ground as Avon came running out of her hiding place.

"What's wrong with Imri?" Avon asked, eyes wide with fright.

"Anger is drawing him toward the dark side of the Force. I have to help him before he gets any worse. You and Jay-Six take care of these guys. And whatever you do, do not follow us."

J-6 opened her chest compartment and pointed a

blaster at both the coughing magenta-haired woman and the unconscious Aqualish man. "If you move, you are dead," she said.

The Nihil woman just coughed more and raised her hands in surrender.

Vernestra gripped her lightsaber and stalked off into the jungle after the Padawan. She would not let Imri fall to the dark side.

Imri groaned as he sat up. Vernestra had thrown him like a child's toy. It was both impressive and infuriating. He was lucky that he had landed on an especially springy patch of ferns, and nothing seemed injured but his pride. She'd overpowered him so easily, but he wouldn't let it happen again.

He would have his vengeance. And if Vernestra tried to stop him she would regret her decision.

Just as Imri drew his lightsaber, Vernestra appeared before him, her green skin bright against the darker coloring of the plants around her. Wisps of hair had come loose from the tie that held it back, and she stood in the ready position with her bright purple lightsaber.

"Imri, stop. You are not going to kill those pirates."

"That's where you're wrong. I am going to kill them. And if you don't let me pass I will kill you first." The words coming from Imri's mouth sounded like someone else's. He didn't really want to kill Vern, did he?

Guilt swept over him. Vernestra had only been kind to him, but there was nothing for him without his master to guide him. He owed it to Douglas to punish the Nihil for their crimes.

So Imri decided he would stand up against Vernestra. He would kill her if she did not let him take care of that despicable human woman and that awful Aqualish man. They did not deserve to live, and he would make certain they did not.

"Move, Vern. I have to do this. For Douglas."

"This is the last thing he would have wanted."

"Move or be moved," Imri said, his voice flat.

Vernestra's expression hardened. "Well then, Padawan. Let's see what you've got."

Imri ignited his lightsaber blade. It was a steady, strong

blue for once, and that gave him confidence. He was as good as Vernestra. He would show her that she had been wrong to underestimate him, just like everyone else.

Then he was charging forward, his anger and the Force propelling him.

Vernestra met his attack easily, and though she was more powerful and better trained, Imri was more than a head taller than her. She said nothing as she fought, her blade striking his again and again as she repelled his attacks. No matter what Imri tried, Vernestra would not yield. So he reached for the Force and pushed.

It did nothing. Vernestra would not be moved.

Her expression hardened, and she leapt into the air and somersaulted backward to avoid his next strike. Imri ran forward, determined to cut the Jedi down, and yelped in surprise as something burned across the back of his hand, causing him to drop his lightsaber.

Vernestra stood before him, her lightsaber transformed into a lightwhip. As Imri reached for his dropped lightsaber, the edge of the lightwhip zipped across the ground, leaving a sizzling groove in the dirt between him and the weapon. Imri tried for his lightsaber once more, but this time Vernestra's whip crackled across the hilt itself, leaving behind two smoking pieces.

"Enough, Imri," Vernestra said. "That's enough. You used the Force in an aggressive manner when you choked that woman! Douglas never would have wanted any of this, especially not Jedi fighting among themselves."

Imri growled in anger at the mention of his dead master. He might not have a lightsaber, but he could still fight. He reached for the Force, but as he did his anger, which had also been fueled by Honesty's rage, began to melt away and he felt for the briefest moment his master's hand resting heavily on his shoulder.

To be a Jedi is to always trust that the Force works in mysterious ways, Imri. We accept and we try our best, but we do not forget that in the end all is as the Force wills it.

Douglas's voice could have been a memory, but it felt like more than that. All the rage drained from Imri and he fell to his knees, burying his face in his hands. He couldn't even sense the anger Honesty had carried, as though the boy had also lost his taste for revenge. He didn't want to cry; he wanted to be angry. But his sadness was more than he could bear and he began to sob.

"It isn't fair. It's not. Douglas was good and kind and strong, and those people killed him. And why? For nothing."

"We're going to find out why, Imri. And you can be angry, but giving in to your rage, letting that single emotion drive your actions, that is a direct path to the dark side. We can bring those people back there to justice, but what that looks like is not up to us. We serve the Force, and the Force does not pick sides."

Vernestra patted Imri once and again before walking over to pick up his broken lightsaber. A deep shame filled Imri. He'd made a mistake, and it was one he would be working to repair for a very long time.

"Come on," Vernestra said. "Let's go find out why those pirates destroyed the *Steady Wing*."

J-6 had just finished tying up the pirates with a complicated series of Batuu knots, something Avon had taught the droid back at Port Haileap, when Vernestra and Imri returned to the ship. The boy looked deflated, and when Avon glanced over at Vernestra with her eyebrows raised in question, Vernestra nodded.

Everything was okay. For now.

Avon gestured to the Aqualish man and human woman where they slumped on the cargo deck inside the ship. They were both conscious, and they glared at the Jedi as they approached.

"I figured tying them up was the safe plan, since I didn't know how long it would be until you got back. Also, I started a distress signal on both Republic and Jedi channels. I sent a general broadcast, as well as one to the temple on Dalna and to Port Haileap. Hopefully someone hears one of them and responds. I would say we should expect a response soon, but in this sector who knows. It could be days or weeks."

"I also sent a message to the Dalnan capital," Honesty said, rubbing the back of his neck. "I figured maybe they could help with the Nihil, since the governor has experience with them." The boy had refused to make eye contact with Avon or speak to her, and she figured it was because he was sore about being saved. How embarrassing to set out to destroy someone only to be taken hostage. He should have assessed his options more logically, but Avon said nothing. She figured hurt pride was enough punishment, although she hoped he'd also realized that maybe violence wasn't always the answer.

Vernestra nodded and pointed for Imri to sit in a corner next to a couple of shipping crates. He did so without a word, and Avon started to walk over to the boy when Vernestra stopped her.

"Leave him be. He has some thinking to do," Vernestra said.

"What happened to him, Vern?" Avon had never seen the boy look as mean as he had when he challenged Vernestra.

"A Jedi must always be vigilant about the lure of the dark side. Imri's grief got the better of him and pushed him into making some regrettable decisions."

Avon looked over at the Padawan and chewed on her bottom lip. "Is he in trouble?"

"I don't know."

"You scruffy mynocks better let us free before we get angry," growled the Aqualish man behind them. Avon and Vernestra turned around, and Vernestra held up a hand as Avon started to take a step forward.

"Allow me," the older girl said, walking toward the bound pirates and crouching down so she was eye level with the Aqualish man.

"Tell me your name," she said, and a funny feeling quivered through Avon. She had the faint urge to tell Vernestra her name, and even as she pushed the feeling aside the man before Vernestra began to speak.

"Gwishi of the Nihil. I am the leader of this Strike."

"Who are the Nihil, exactly? Are you just pirates?" Avon asked, preempting Vernestra's question. Whatever Vernestra was doing to make the man cooperate was still working. He drew his shoulders back as he sat up straighter.

"We are more powerful than that. Pirates wish they could do what we do. The Nihil go where they want, do what they want, and take whatever they want. We are many, and we are strong, and only the strongest shall survive, as it was always meant to be."

Vernestra tilted her head. "So why did you destroy the *Steady Wing*? What did the ship have that you wanted?"

Gwishi said nothing, merely shook his head. Vernestra waved her hand before his eyes slowly and repeated her question. But the Aqualish man refused to answer.

"We didn't want Dalna to join the Republic," the woman behind him answered. Gwishi swore in Aqualish, and J-6 chuckled.

"That was a particularly good one. Would you like me to translate?"

"No," said Vernestra at the same time Avon said, "Yes!" Avon was about to argue, but a stern look from the Jedi had her clamping her lips together and raising her hands in surrender.

"Why didn't you want Dalna to join the Republic?" Honesty said, seemingly out of nowhere. He walked over to the woman, who glared at him in defiance.

"Because this is *our* sector. If we have Republic cruisers patrolling this part of space it will ruin everything. And now that the Nihil are at war with the Jedi and the Republic, you're going to feel the true depths of our wrath. A storm is coming, and you will regret standing against us. The strong survive, the weak die."

Honesty looked at the woman for a very long time before nodding. "Well, then we are just going to have to stop you so that you never get to hurt anyone else." He turned and walked back toward the cargo hold and sat down on a crate. Avon looked at Vernestra before walking over to the boy and sitting next to him.

"I'm sorry about your father," she said, unsure what to do but settling for an awkward pat of his knee.

"Do you think your mother could get me an audience with the Senate?" he asked after a very long time.

"I don't know, maybe. Why?"

"Because, I want to be there firsthand to tell them what these Nihil or whatever did to my father and my friends." A tear slid down the boy's cheek, and Avon wrapped her arms around his unyielding frame, giving what comfort she could.

"Honesty, I will make sure you get to talk to the Senate no matter what. I promise."

And then there was nothing but silence for a very long time. But when he hugged her back Avon realized that they'd somehow become friends, and that just made her embrace the boy a little harder.

⬥

Two days after their group took the Nihil saboteurs hostage, the Jedi came to save Avon, Imri, Honesty, and Vernestra. It had been a quiet, fraught couple of days. During the wait SD-7's battery had finally given out, and Avon sadly tucked him into her pack, making a note to carry extra batteries in the future. J-6 did not need to sleep, and she was able to charge herself by way of a charge port in the ship, so she paced around the Nihil with her blasters drawn, firing a warning shot into the air every time they looked a little too comfortable and taking a bit more joy in the shooting than Avon was comfortable with.

She was going to have to calibrate J-6's programming *just a bit* when they got back to civilization. Not enough to make her like she used to be, but definitely enough to make sure she didn't get too blasty at the wrong moment.

The Jedi who found them were a Trandoshan, Master Sskeer, and his Padawan learner, Keeve Trennis, both on their way back from the planet Shuraden. Avon was giddy as they stepped into the clearing, Republic security forces following him. The Jedi Master was missing an arm, and Avon burned with a need to know how he had lost it. "Do you know Trandoshans can regenerate body parts?" she whisper-yelled to Honesty, who was so accustomed to Avon's spontaneous lectures by then that he just gave her a small smile.

"Please do not start asking the Jedi Master about his missing body parts," Vernestra said, her ability to read Avon more annoying than anything else.

"I wasn't. I was just going to ask him how long it will take to grow back." But the Mirialan was already moving toward their rescuer.

Avon walked over to where Imri sat in a back corner of the Nihil ship. The boy had barely spoken since his fight with Vernestra, and when he did speak there was a hesitancy to his words, as though he feared them and what he might say. While J-6 had been tasked with keeping track of the Nihil prisoners, Vernestra had watched Imri just as closely, so that Honesty and Avon were left wondering what had transpired between the two of them. Avon knew it had something to do with being a Jedi, something about the dark side and how Jedi could become bad if they lost their way, but she still wasn't certain of the details. And Vernestra had made sure that Avon couldn't find out what had happened.

Vernestra was talking to the Jedi Master, and Avon would only have a short time to talk to the boy.

"So, I guess this is the last time we'll get to hang out," she said, sitting down next to him. "Seems like you're in pretty big trouble."

"That's putting it lightly," he said.

"What happened to you?"

Imri shrugged. "A Jedi is supposed to understand that hate and anger are too destructive to be nursed for long.

I forgot that, and it kind of led me to make some terrible decisions."

"Like trying to fight Vern?"

Imri actually smiled. "Yeah, that was dumb."

Avon sighed. "Everyone makes mistakes. They're not going to kick you out of the Jedi for that, are they?"

Imri shook his head. "No, I don't think so. Vern seems to think I'll have to go back and spend some time in one of the temples, repeat some of my training. But I don't know if I want to do that, either." Imri blinked hard, like he was fighting back tears. "I don't think I'm cut out to be a Jedi."

"*Pffft*, nonsense." Avon bumped her shoulder against the much larger boy's. "When I arrived at Port Haileap no one worked harder to make me feel welcome than you did. You're a good person, Imri. The Jedi are lucky to have you."

He sniffed and nodded. "Thanks, Avon. I appreciate that."

"Also, if you want I can hold on to your lightsaber for you, just until you're better."

Imri laughed. "I don't even have it. Vern took it after we fought. Besides, the thing is broken. It's completely useless."

Avon's heart leapt in both excitement and despair. She

hadn't really expected Imri to say yes, but she also hadn't expected to get a broken lightsaber. This was the best of all possibilities. If no one was looking for the lightsaber, no one would be missing the lightsaber.

So when Vernestra was distracted with the newly arrived Jedi Master and Honesty was talking to Imri and J-6 was waiting for a chance to shoot the Nihil, Avon scurried over to Vernestra's pack.

One day, science would thank her for her questionable behavior. Avon was certain of it.

As more and more Jedi arrived, cutting their way through the jungle and eventually bringing in a cargo speeder to get everyone back to their ship, Avon very quietly found the pieces of Imri's lightsaber in Vernestra's pack. She slipped them into her own knapsack right next to the powered-down SD and a single leftover packet of joppa stew.

Overall, not a terrible adventure.

Vernestra looked out one of the many observation windows on Starlight Beacon. They had arrived in time for the dedication. They'd made good time from the Haileap system, less than two days, and that had required a couple of lightspeed skips as they navigated lanes that had not been impacted by the recent disaster. Reports stated that the Jedi were still responding to Emergences, but the worst of the catastrophe was past them.

As they'd approached the station, it shone like a benevolent star, the white glow warm and welcoming. The central spire blinked in a slow array of rainbow colors, and ships approached in organized lines, following predesignated lanes. The space station would increase communication, provide a waypoint for weary travelers, and help the Jedi carry out their missions of peace. Everything about it had been chosen with the majesty of the Republic and the light of the Jedi in mind, and just seeing it helped ease some of Vernestra's doubts and fears. She would never be Master Douglas, but she could try her best, just like she always had.

As for the rest of their group, Vernestra had no doubts that things would be fine. Avon and Honesty had already announced that they planned on seeing every centimeter of the marvel of Starlight Beacon before they left, and they would have some time to do just that. Vernestra was calm and at peace. They had survived the destruction of the *Steady Wing* and captured those responsible for the loss. Honesty would plead his case in an address to the Senate, and Avon was excited to spend some time in the research labs on Starlight before going back to Port Haileap.

But Vernestra could not find any joy in the outcome. All she could see was the fervent way the Nihil had spoken about waging war against the Jedi, their conviction that they could do as they pleased, even going so far as to sabotage innocent civilians. Hundreds had been lost with the *Steady Wing*, and those deaths would reverberate throughout the galaxy, stoking fear and anger. Even though the Republic and Dalna would respond, they would look to the Jedi for help. It was what the Jedi did, and Vernestra vowed she would be ready when she was called. That tempered any joy Vernestra might have felt at being off Wevo and back to civilization.

Plus, there was still the matter of Imri. What would become of the Padawan with no master?

"You are uneasy, Vernestra." The words were spoken with a hiss, which meant the voice could only belong to one person.

She turned around to find Master Sskeer standing in the doorway to the observation chamber. She gave him a smile and turned away from the window to walk toward him. She'd found the Jedi Master's guidance to be helpful and calming, and even though she had thought herself past the need for such direction, she knew that it was still helpful to have someone to talk to.

"I am worried about Imri," Vernestra said with a sigh. The Padawan had become even more withdrawn since they'd boarded the *Radiant Blessing* back on Wevo, and no one had been able to get through to him. He'd locked himself away emotionally and Vernestra was worried that the Order would lose him.

"Then you should take the boy as your Padawan," Master Sskeer said. His calm suggestion hit Vernestra like a sack of droid parts.

"What? What are you talking about? I already let Imri down on Wevo. If I had been better prepared he never would have given in so completely to anger. He could have gone to the dark side."

The Jedi Master chuckled a little. "The Force is not so simple, and neither are the emotions of living creatures. Most Jedi have felt the temptation of the dark side. It is only natural. But we resist it. It is a deliberate path to the dark, not a series of bad days. Being a Jedi is about choosing the light over and over again."

Vernestra heaved a sigh. "I know this, deep down. But I don't know how to teach that to Imri when he's so filled with doubt."

Master Sskeer held out his hand in supplication. "Imri was able to find his way back to the light with your help, Vernestra. Only yours. You are a fully accomplished Knight, and taking a Padawan is something you will be expected to do. So why not now?"

"I will think on it."

"Ah, and now you are driven by your own doubts."

Vernestra laughed. "I guess I am."

They stared out the observation window, at the light that shone from the top of the Beacon.

Vernestra excused herself and went to find Imri. She could sense him in the meditation garden, and she found him sitting on a bench next to a pond filled with biolumi-nescent fish that sang their joy through the living Force as they swam. It was a lovely sound, and Vernestra could not help smiling at their elation.

As she entered the garden Imri's head jerked up guiltily. "Am I in trouble?"

Vernestra frowned. "What would make you think that?"

"I could sense you thinking about me, but the emotions are a tangle. I figured I was finally going to be in trouble."

Vernestra shook her head and sat next to Imri on the

bench. "No, you're not in trouble. I told you before that there would be no punishment for what happened on Wevo."

"But I embraced Honesty's anger, letting it fuel my own, and fought with you. That was so wrong."

"Recognizing our mistakes and doing better is the path of a Jedi. Imri, the Jedi Order isn't going to kick you out for a single mistake. It just doesn't work that way. If it did there wouldn't be anyone left. I was scared on Wevo because I didn't think I could help you, and I was afraid to reach out the way I wanted to. But I think now that we could work well together. I'd like you to be my Padawan if that wouldn't be too weird." When Imri didn't say anything, Vernestra gave him a hopeful smile. "I'm not Master Douglas, but he was right about you: you're going to make an amazing Jedi one day, because you are willing to adapt and change."

"Do you really mean it?" Tears streamed down the boy's pale cheeks, and Vernestra wrapped an arm around his shoulders.

"Of course. We can start your training right after the dedication is completed."

CHAPTER TWENTY-THREE

Imri nodded, smiling for the first time in days. "I won't let you down."

"I know you won't," Vernestra said with an answering smile.

They sat in the garden a few moments more before Imri asked Vernestra, "Do you think we should be worried about the Nihil?"

Vernestra didn't say anything for a long time, but then she took a deep breath and let it out slowly. "I think we have seen only the least of what they are capable of, Imri. But don't worry. We're Jedi. We'll be ready when next they strike."

EPILOGUE

Kara Xoo leaned back in the command chair of her ship, the *Poisoned Barb*. She looked at the holo and gnashed her teeth. It was from a week before, from the far edge of the Haileap system. In it Klinith Da, one of Kara's least favorite humans, talked too fast and looked more than a little scared. If the woman had been a proper Quarren like Kara she would have known how to hold herself to look fierce. Instead every emotion flickered across Klinith's face, making her look less like a Nihil and more like prey.

"We have been stranded on a small moon that we've

identified as Wevo. I'm pretty sure it's cursed, but Gwishi says it's just because there are a couple of Jedi kids here. We're going to take care of them, don't worry. The *Steady Wing* massacre will look like just another dangerous hyperspace accident. No witnesses, no problem."

Kara turned toward the Weequay standing nearby. She couldn't remember the little grunt's name, and she didn't try. He was only in her command room because he'd been part of the Strike sent to find Gwishi and Klinith.

"You're sure there was no sign of them?" Kara asked.

The Weequay nodded. "Just the smashed remnants of that ship we helped them steal before they left."

"Fine. Get out."

Kara stood and swallowed a curse. Like most Nihil in her Storm, she wore a tunic and trousers with heavy magboots, all black, all of it stolen along the way. She had lost one of her face tentacles in a recent battle; the glistening tip showed blue, the only hint of color on her besides the reddish-brown of her skin. She knew she made an imposing figure, especially when she stood, and the nervousness of the Weequay as he scuttled away gave her a measure of joy.

She waited until the grunt had left before she started pacing. It would do no good for the small fry to see her nervous. Klinith and Gwishi were the seventh Strike Kara had lost in as many days. She'd sent a large measure of her forces to Kassav as he had requested, and she had heard nothing from them, either. No Strikes meant that her Storm was losing strength, and when they looked weak one of the other Storms would move in to destroy them.

That was the way of the Nihil.

Kara had to do something, and she stroked one of her tentacles as she walked. She needed to increase her numbers, and fast, anything to make her Storm look less vulnerable. They'd tried recruiting the normal way, through scouting cantinas and straightforward fear, but it was slow going and Kara needed a way to increase her fighting force faster.

There are a couple of Jedi kids here. . . .

Kara blinked as the idea blossomed in her mind, and she went to her command chair and pushed a call button. "Pere, how many schools are there on Dalna?"

There was a burst of static before the answer came across the comlink. "Um, maybe a hundred or so? Why?"

Kara sat back in her chair. If she could grin like a

human she would, but instead she let her face tentacles dance. "We have some recruiting to do."

She would show the Republic and the Jedi just what the Nihil were capable of. Kassav and the other Tempest Runners would be proud. And when she was done, the Dalnan sector would be nothing but ashes.

ABOUT THE
AUTHOR

Justina Ireland is the author of *Dread Nation*, a *New York Times* best seller and YALSA 2019 Best Fiction for Young Adults Top Ten selection. Her other books for children and teens include *Deathless Divide*, *Vengeance Bound*, *Promise of Shadows*, and the *Star Wars* novels *Lando's Luck* and *Spark of the Resistance*. She enjoys dark chocolate and dark humor and is not too proud to admit that she's still afraid of the dark. She lives with her husband, kid, dog, and cats in Maryland. You can visit her online at www.justinaireland.com.

READ ON FOR A SNEAK PEEK AT ANOTHER
EXCITING HIGH REPUBLIC ADVENTURE,
COMING IN JULY 2021!

RACE to CRASHPOINT TOWER

DANIEL JOSÉ OLDER

PART
ONE

Floating a half meter above an old starfighter pilot seat, Ram Jomaram closed his eyes and tried to block out all the clatter and commotion outside. There was plenty to block out: dignitaries and visitors from the entire known galaxy were converging on the scenic mountains and forests of Valo for the first Republic Fair in ages. Most of Valo City's residents were putting final touches on banners, cooking scrumptious food, and preparing guest quarters. Pretty soon they'd be getting ready to gather at the almost fully constructed Jedi temple for the opening convocation.

But!

None of that mattered.

All that mattered was this very moment.

Ram had slyly mentioned to Master Kunpar that one of the security team's speeder bikes was out of commission with a faulty gasket hub, and all the state mechanics were busy setting up the light show, sooooo . . . Master Kunpar had grumbled and fussed with his chin tentacles some before finally relenting, but he had, and that's why Ram got to be in his favorite place on the planet: a dingy, dim garage full of rusty mechanical parts and tools.

The team of repair Bonbraks scurried back and forth on the shelves around him, chattering at each other and futzing with various smaller projects, but otherwise, Jedi Padawan Ram Jomaram was in the most peaceful state he knew: all alone in his garage.

No complicated rules or protocols to follow, no ancient wise Masters to show the correct deference to. Just metal and bolts and plastic and some big-eared, long-tailed fur balls who made plenty of squeaky fuss but mostly minded their own business.

Ram was one with the Force, and the Force was with Ram, he reminded himself. Here, in this peaceful, grease-stained hideaway, he could give over fully to the quiet, powerful place inside. All around him, a small constellation of speeder parts hovered. There was the leather seat and metal casing over the main hub—he could swing those out of the way for the moment. Here was the engine, with its grill and gaskets and piping. Here was the fuse box that would fit in alongside the fan belt and connect into the rest of the machinery. And there was the repulsor lift hub, still shiny with residue from when it had spluttered fission oil earlier during a routine patrol.

Ram could feel the quiet thrum of each part, the tiny vibrations in the air that described them as they floated in a slow circle around him, that faraway trill within the hub that rang just a fraction of a note dissonant from the rest of the parts. There! That meant something was off. Something had warped the shape of it, probably too much heat, but how? Something else must be wrong. Ram continued the scan, his mind sliding along the accelerator foot pedals, steering mechanism, control panels, and exhaust pipe. He had just caught the faintest sense of something, a teensy, off-key ding, when—

"GREETINGS, MASTER RAM!" the metallic voice of V-18 called from the doorway.

"I am one with the Force and the Force is with me," Ram whispered, eyes still closed. The speeder parts faltered in their slow rotation, dipped toward the ground.

"*JomaramaRam do chunda mota mota-ta!*" an irritated Bonbrak countered. That was probably Tip, the youngest and surliest of the crew. Several others concurred loudly.

"Well, there's no need to be rude," V-18 said.

The speeder parts slid lower. "I am one with the Force and the Force is with me," Ram growled.

"*Bacha no bacha kribkrib patrak!*"

"*Pratrak patrak!*"

"*JomaramaRam!*"

"I simply expressed my salutations," V-18 insisted. "I happen to be both excited to see the young Padawan and on an errand of some urgency, which is why I modulated my voice into a higher frequency and volume, for your info—"

One of the Bonbraks grunted out a squeak (almost definitely Fezmix—he was always the rowdy one), and then a metallic *ding!* rang out and V-18 yelped.

"Unnecessary!" cried the droid.

"I AM ONE WITH THE FORCE AND THE FORCE IS WITH ME!" Ram hollered as all the speeder parts except one clattered to the floor. He looked up to see seven pairs of black beady eyes and one glowing electronic one staring back at him.

"Oh dear," muttered V-18.

Ram sighed, and then the last piece landed with a *clank!*

The Bonbraks immediately began bickering among themselves, and Ram lowered his legs onto the pilot seat and rubbed his eyes. "What is it, Vee-Eighteen?"

The droid had been around for Force knew how many years and it showed. He towered over everyone like a big, ridiculous rusty crate with stumpy legs. Ram had had to paint him bright purple because people kept accidentally loading V-18 onto ships when he was in sleep mode, thinking he was cargo. A single off-center eye glared out of each side and sometimes blinked, which either indicated impatience or a programming glitch—Ram was never sure. "Masters Kunpar and Lege are on a routine check of the lake," V-18 announced.

"Okay?"

"And Masters Devo and Shonnatrucks are greeting some of the new security forces the Republic has sent for the fair."

"Vee-Eighteen . . ."

"And all the other Padawans are with them."

"Vee-Eighteen, why are you telling me the location of all the Valorian Jedi?"

"Because the comms tower is glitchy."

The comms tower was outside Valo City proper, deep in the Farodin Woods. And it would be dark soon. "Well, I better take a look at it."

"No!"

Ram blinked at V-18. "Why not?"

"Because there's a matter that requires your attention more urgently," the droid said.

"Are you going to make me take you apart to access your databanks for it or are you just going to tell me what it is?"

"My, my! There's no need to—"

"Vee-Eighteen!"

"There was an alert tripped on the security perimeter of the comms tower."

Ram's eyes went wide. "Crashpoint Tower?"

"Uh, that's not the official name, but I suppose so, yes."

A perimeter breach wasn't necessarily a big deal— probably just some forest critter. But with the Nihil attacks in the Outer Rim and the fair coming up, everyone was on high alert, so the Jedi had been instructed to treat any possible security issue as top priority. "What? Did you alert the Masters?"

V-18 shook his big boxy body and blinked irritably—this time Ram was positive that flicker was on purpose. "I just told you! The comms are glitchy! Sheesh, man!"

"So there's a security breach at the comms tower, and the comms are glitchy? And . . . Why didn't you tell me that in the first place?"

"Well, I didn't want anyone to get hurt."

Ram didn't have time to get into all the ways that didn't make sense. "We have to get out there! When was the breach?"

"One hour ago!" V-18 announced triumphantly.

"We have to go now! We gotta—" He spun around, ready to jump on the security speeder bike, and then remembered that it was in pieces all over the garage floor. And he wasn't cleared to use any of the larger transports. And walking would take too long—they'd never make it before dark, and whatever had breached the perimeter and possibly damaged the comms tower would be long gone. Which might be a good thing, because then Ram wouldn't have to confront them and maybe fight with them. Ram hated fighting. Well—he'd never done it, but he hated the idea of it. It felt like his body refused to cooperate any time even a practice battle was called for. Lightsaber Training and General Jedi Combat Maneuvers were his two worst classes, and the very thought of going face to face with an enemy made him jittery.

But it didn't matter. He was a Jedi Padawan and he was apparently the only one around to deal with this. It was his duty, even he if would've rather spent the rest of the night tinkering. That meant he had to get out there as fast as possible.

He eyed V-18.

"First I had to go see where the Jedi Masters were, according to protocol," the droid rambled, "but the living quarters and temple were both empty! And then I tried to raise them on the comms but . . . why are you looking at me like that?"

An idea formulated inside Ram, and once that happened,

it was hard to think of anything else. He was probably squinting creepily at the droid; he was definitely assessing where different parts could fit on that bulky frame. "Do those legs retract?" Ram glanced at a spare propulsor unit he'd nabbed off an old single-pilot crop sifter headed for the junk pile. Seven tiny pairs of eyes followed his gaze.

"I'll have you know that this nimble but robust physique is capable of an unpredictable number of—"

"Do they retract?" Ram shot a meaningful glance at the Bonbraks, who'd already started moving into position around V-18. He was glad they'd learned to recognize his about-to-spring-into-action face.

"Of course! No need to interr—"

"How would you feel about a mobility upgrade?"

"Well, I hardly see how you could upgrade this unparalleled appara—"

"Vee-Eighteen!"

"Why, yes actually, I would like that quite a bit," the droid admitted.

"Let's do it!" Ram yelled, and with high-pitched squeals, the Bonbraks pounced.

"What's going on?" V-18 wailed. "Unhand me, you tiny

vagrants! You're getting greasy little fingerprints on my delicate firmament!"

"This won't take long," Ram assured him.

It didn't. V-18 got enthusiastic quickly once he realized how cool the upgrade was going to be, and even tried to help out some. With the Bonbraks running point on the wiring and fuses, Ram secured the propulsor to V-18 and rigged up a handy saddle with foot pedals to control acceleration. There wasn't time to add brakes, but who needed brakes, right? Okay—he did eventually, but he'd have to work that out later. For now, decelerating would have to do.

He shot a wistful glance at the scattered remains of the speeder, then used a foot pedal to heave himself onto V-18. The seat they'd attached was pretty comfy, and the handlebars reached up to just the right height. Ram revved the engine once and then whooshed out the door to the cheers of the Bonbraks.

"This is actually quite enjoyable!" V-18 yelled over the whistling wind as they zoomed past the shacks on the outskirts of Valo City and into the Farodin Woods.

"I thought you might like it," Ram said. "The question is, can we go any faster . . . ?"

"I'm not sure that's—"

Ram pushed the accelerator pedal all the way down and V-18 lurched into overdrive, flashing around the towering acthorn trees, then zipping up a hill and over a rocky embankment. "Wooooooooooooohooooooooo!" Ram yelled.

The sun was just starting to dip into the clouds over the distant mountain range as they burst out above the field where Crashpoint Tower was.

Ram pulled his foot off the accelerator. Something moved in the clearing ahead: a figure, standing up from where it had been crouching, then raising a long cylinder. Ram's eyes went wide. He swung hard on the throttle and gunned the thrusters just as the first blast of cannon fire smashed through the trees behind him.

"Yeeeeeeeeeee!" V-18 screeched. Another fiery shot tore over their heads. "What do we do now?"

Ram pulled them behind a pile of boulders and eased into a hover. The shooting had stopped, but he could hear the angry growls of speeder engines. Way up past the branches and leaves, a few tiny lights blinked against the darkening sky. "They're going to make a run for it," Ram whispered. "Back to whatever ship brought them here." If they were more interested in getting away than finishing off Ram, that meant whatever they were hiding was very important indeed. Which meant—

"I hope you're not planning to—" V-18 warned just as Ram revved up the engine.

"We gotta stop them!"